Standing in Shadows

STANDING IN SHADOWS

Dark Fey Book II

Cynthia A. Morgan

Copyright (C) 2015 Cynthia A. Morgan
Layout design and Copyright (C) 2020 by Next Chapter
Published 2020 by Shadow City – A Next Chapter Imprint
Cover art by Cover Mint
This book is a work of fiction. Names, characters, places, and incidents are the product of the author's imagination or are used fictitiously. Any resemblance to actual events, locales, or persons, living or dead, is purely coincidental.
All rights reserved. No part of this book may be reproduced or transmitted in any form or by any means, electronic or mechanical, including photocopying, recording, or by any information storage and retrieval system, without the author's permission.

*Dedicated to my Loving Family and Friends
Who have supported me and my writing
For many years*

And

*In Special Remembrance of my Mother,
Whose Love, Hope and Joy Inspired Every day.*

*And
For the Love of the Muse…*

An Introduction to Dark Fey Standing in Shadows

Book one, Dark Fey: The Reviled began the journey, introducing us to the Mystical Realm of Jyndari, the home of the Fey of the Light who are winged beings with extraordinary gifts and abilities. They live harmoniously in a close knit community where art and music, scholarly devotion to the ancient texts, and faithful adherence to tradition are all sacred. In Jyndari we meet a young Fey of the Light, Ayla who was discovered at a very young age to have the especially rare combination of gifts: empathic telepathy as well as discernment and healing. She was dedicated to become a Guardian of Childfey and spent her entire young years in the seclusion of the Temple where she studied magic and the ancient rites; where she was taught about the mortal enemy of all Fey of the Light, The Reviled.

We also meet Gairynzvl, a Reviled Fey who comes in shadows and silence; who lingers near Ayla trying to communicate with her. He longs for freedom from his captivity among the Dark Fey, but he needs her help to escape them. Through her extraordinary gifts she listens to him when no others will; she touches his pain and eases his suffering and she helps him in his attempt to escape The Reviled.

Known also as The Cursed, the Dark Ones or The Reviled Fey cannot love, are unable to abide peace or harmony, and do not admire beauty or talent without avarice. Because of their cursed state, they also cannot bring life into the world in the form of Innocence. In order to reproduce themselves they come to Jyndari in the shadows and abduct childfey, returning them to their own dark realm, the Uunglarda, where they are forced to endure The Integration. The intentionally cruel process of neglect, abuse and deprivation is designed to turn childfey from the Light and twist them into monsters.

In Dark Fey: Standing in Shadows we discover more about Gairynzvl and why he wants to return into the dark realm of The Reviled. He longs to attempt a rescue of the innocent childfey trapped there!

But it will take more than one Fey to breach the borders of The Uunglarda and to slip past the legions of Dark Fey who abide there. It will take magic and strength, courage and military strategy and it will shake the foundations of everything The Fey of The Light have accepted as truth for thousands of years. Nevertheless, Gairynzvl knows the secret ways in and out of the dark realm; he is able to open portals and through his gifts of telepathic empathy, he can find the childfey standing, waiting, in the shadows.

Slipping into the darkness through darkness is easy. Escaping out again with squalling, terrified childfey is another matter, but if they are captured his band of Liberators will pray for death long before it comes. Worse, their success could spark full scale war and unleash the barbaric hatred and viciousness of The Reviled upon the peace-loving Fey of The Light.

Can Gairynzvl convince Ayla and The Temple Elders to allow him to return to the Uunglarda, the realm of The Reviled? Who will join him to aid these Innocent Childfey, trapped in the realm of shadows and fear? And Will the Fey of the Light risk a savage war in order to rescue them?

A Word about Fey Words

Celebrae is the ancient, root language of the Fey of the Light. It is a gentle, elegant language filled with soft sounds spoken upon the tip of the tongue and pronounced near the front of the mouth. As a result is it often quiet in tone or light in inflection. Its vowel sounds are clear and crisp as well as delicate and lush.

- Nearly all R's are trilled in both High Celebrae and the common tongue, most especially in instances of names of malefey.

- The letter Y is generally pronounced like a short I, as in the words: with, dish, visit. OR Veryn Falls, Jyndari, Veryth.

- When the letter Y follows the letter A it is pronounced like a long A, as in the words: Pray, Brave, Stay OR Ayla, Nayina, Luxay.

- When the letter Y is followed immediately by another letter Y, it is pronounced like a long E, as in the words: Free, See, Three OR Suubsyydd and Ryydde,

- The letters AE, when found together, are pronounced like a long A, as in the words: Lay, Say, Engrave OR Rehstaed, Celebrae, Jocyndrae Vite.

- The letters AU, when found together, are pronounced like AW, as in the words: Saw, Flaw, Draw OR as in the phrase Luxaunyth sha-lindauwyn. Vas hevauthycaera.

- When the letter U is followed immediately by another U, it is pronounced like OO, though a soft repetition of the sound occurs, as in the words: Soon, Bloom, Doom OR Uunglarda and Suubsyydd.

- DD is pronounced like soft TH, as in the words: Bath, Math, Path OR Suubsyydd and Ryydde.

- NN is pronounced just the same as a single N and AA is pronounced as a short A, as in Father, Hall, Ball, but a soft repetition of the sound occurs.

In contrast to the Light, Bright and Beautiful language of the Fey of the Light, the language of The Reviled or Dlalth is filled with guttural vocalizations characterized by harsh and grating sounds made in the throat or toward the back of the mouth. Since all Reviled Fey were once Fey of the Light, many similarities still exist between the languages, such as the pronunciation of Y, DD, NN and trilled R's, with the distinction coming in the manner of how the sounds are produced. Where Celebrae is soft and elegant, Dlalth is harsh and guttural. Many Dlalth words also contain more consonants than vowels, creating words that are severe and vile to the ear. Some examples of pronunciation would be:

- The letter H is not a soft sound, as in the words: Happy, House, Harmony, but instead the letter H is formed in the back of the throat, creating more of a throaty hissing sound. Hravclanoch would have the accent on the harsh, guttural H.

- The letters CH are not pronounced crisp and clear, as in the words: Chirp, Starch, Reach, but instead the sound is formed near the back of the mouth, creating the sound more frequently associated with the Scottish CH in the word Loch or the German CH in the word Bach. Hravclanoch not only has the accent on the harsh, guttural H, but the gravelly CH at the end of the word.

- AA is pronounced like a short A, such as in the words: Father, Hall, Ball, though the sound originates closer to the back of the mouth and a soft repetition of the sound occurs. The Dlalth curse, Raach, would be pronounced with a trilled R, ah, ah, and a gravelly CH.

- Combinations of consonant sounds are often utilized to form vulgar, throaty sounding words, such as HR, where the R cannot be trilled, but when combined with the deep throaty hiss of the H the sound becomes more harsh than either letter alone. Another example of odd combinations is Hrch, Lych, and Zvl, where the sound of each individual letter is blended into the next, forming an abrasive, snarling, and gravelly sound.

Chapter One

Darkness lay thick and unyielding like a heavy mantle that smothered from every direction at once. Pungent and prodding, the intense murk was sooty with the condensing smoke of a thousand fires, which was the only source of light permitted in the, otherwise, bleak city. As it curled in the streets and avenues, turning frequented ways into misleading paths that made even those most familiar with them turn about more than once to reorient themselves, layers of damp mist leached downward from the leaden sky. Out of the dimness that poured from the ashen buildings and sank from above, voices of discontent and misery echoed among the shadows. Unmistakable cries of torment serrated the dense atmosphere; yet, from those same environs, delirious laughter also careened into the brooding night. The opposing sounds confused the ear and twisted the heart with uncertainty and dread.

The city was rank with a foul odor that was sour and reeked of sulfur. It was the city's chief source of kindling that burned in grates and braziers. Drawing close to these fires in order to escape the permeating cold and extract some meager warmth or to find any sense of direction also meant breathing in the malodorous stench that twisted the stomach until it could be born no longer and chased the one seeking momentary solace back into the shadows. There was little warmth in the darkness. An unshakable, seeking chill melted through clothes regardless of the protection of layers. In the ominous gloom, buildings seemed to press together to stay warm, their misaligned, shoddy workmanship betraying their untended state. Some leaned precariously, some were half fallen over in tatters, some were little more than a collapsed hovel and on every street raucous taverns and brothels tainted the air with lascivious noise and drunken abandon.

Standing In Shadows

Through the curling shadows and dusky fog, a willowy, silent figure moved. Draped in an obscuring confusion of shadow that it seemed to carry along with it, the figure stole silently down the street. Muffled by the thick smog that twisted in the air, the form made no sound whatsoever, but drifted past the raucous taverns and foul brothels like a ghost brazenly wandering through the haze. None who passed this cloaked figure took notice of it. No heads turned as it paused at the corner beneath a spluttering lamp of burning, sulfurous, gas. Not a single bystander gazed in its direction as it moved silently down the narrow street towards the edge of town and when it turned the corner, disappearing into the blackness like a shadow melting into graying twilight, no trace of its passage was left behind.

Turning the darkened corner, the ebon shadow paused, the silhouette of its garments contracting as if the figure were doubling over and a muffled sound, like that of despair, slipped outward into the murk. Silence greeted this hushed cry, but as if in echo, a child's wail pierced the heavy gloom. The keening sound was not close by, yet it pealed through the dismal atmosphere like the sharp clangor of a tolling bell and all who heard it shrank from the sound, stifling the evidence of such misery in whatever escape lay close at hand. The amber liquid contained within a bottle, the glittering secret injected directly into veins, or the fleeting, wanton embrace that left a deeper yearning than what it satisfied were momentary releases from the anguish of everyday life.

As the half seen figure stood motionless, the piteous sounds of the city gathered around it like moths drawn to an open flame demanding to be noticed in spite of the listener's desire for deafness. Reality in the Uunglarda was caustic as acid and burned just as deeply and it compelled the figure to move hastily onward.

* * *

Ayla stood silently, her thoughts tumbling in a thousand directions as she gazed down upon Mardan who was still sleeping in the Nursing Ward. Beside her, his own thoughts predictably restive, Gairynzvl did not speak, but waited as patiently as his agitation would allow while she attempted to reach out to their unconscious friend. Tears threatened to prevail over her chaotic emotions as she stretched forth her senses into the peaceful void of Mardan's essence. She anticipated touching nothingness, darkness, and quietness, but her acute senses were met with the gentlest of thoughts. Gasping aloud, she opened her eyes to stare down at him with exhilaration thrilling through her, waiting expectantly for him to pierce her with his brilliant cerulean gaze, but he remained asleep.

Gairynzvl turned to watch more attentively, his unspoken questions about their friend answered by a flurry of excited emotion and confusion that poured from Ayla unchecked. Her emotions fluttered briefly, but she refocused her attention and tried again when one of the Healers drew closer. He watched curiously with a penetrating viridian gaze as she closed her eyes and reached to touch Mardan upon his chest so she could feel the strong, rhythmic beat of his heart and sense the pulse of his essence. Where she could perceive only frightful stillness the day before, she could now hear the soft notions of his dreams. Where terrifying weakness had been present only hours before, she could now feel the strengthening rush of life-force returning within him and she could not contain her elation at the discovery. Drawing back from the light touch she had extended, she muffled a prodigious sob and burst into tears.

"What do you sense, Ayla?" Gairynzvl asked softly, moving to draw her into an embrace even as the Healer stepped forward to check Mardan's condition for himself. She shook her head, delighted, although observably confounded.

"He remains adrift, but I feel strength returning to him. I can hear his thoughts again, though they are quiet." Gazing down on him, she smiled amidst her tears. "He is dreaming."

Gairynzvl turned to look down at Mardan with an unexpected feeling of relief. Although it had been only days since the motionless Celebrant had tried to kill him with the spell of Inflicted Pain, he could not deny that he was pleased he would survive. He watched him curiously, wondering about the depth of his sleep and how it had restored him, but his attention was diverted by the noise of Ayla's piercing confusion and he turned to look down at her with an unreadable expression. "Why, then, are you perplexed?" he asked bluntly, a familiar rush of agitation with her perpetually swirling emotions replacing the brief moment of thankfulness he experienced at her unexpected discovery. Twisting away from him, she rebuked him sharply.

"Stop reading me without my permission!" Her caustic tone made him flinch and step back. Their agitated tones caused the Healer to pause and look up at them uncertainly, although he did not withdraw, and Gairynzvl shook his head.

"I am not reading you Ayla. Anyone can see that you are confused, but you cannot blame me for hearing your thoughts." Before he could complete his sentence, she reproached him again.

"You are always reading them!" she accused vehemently, but her anger only served to annoy him further. Arching his wings aggressively, he stepped forward confrontationally. Staring down into her upturned face with a potent combination of indignation and unanticipated desire he spoke slowly in a low and measured tone as he explained what she already knew perfectly well.

"I have not had the training you have, Ayla. I cannot help hearing the thoughts of others or sensing what they feel. Most of this constant noise I have learned to shut out, but how can I keep myself from hearing you when you are constantly shouting your thoughts at me."

She stared back at him crossly, but the tears in her amber eyes betrayed her frustration and after a tense moment of awkward silence she looked away from him and back at Mardan who lay quiet and unmoving. "I thought…" her voice trailed off as her musings tumbled chaotically. Images played through her mind of piercing cerulean eyes watching her from the shadows outside the Chamber of Radiance and of intense jealousy and loathing. Unable to block the sudden onslaught of these emotions, Gairynzvl turned his head to the side, his tone more quiet, but no less imposing as he queried further.

"What did you think?"

She sighed sharply and closed her eyes, attempting for the first time in a very long time to reign in her wildly conflicting sentiments. Regardless of her attempts, however, she knew he could read her as easily as he could the open sky and this realization only flustered her further. "Please, Gairynzvl, do not."

At this, the Healer lifted his head to watch them more intently, ready to defend her, if necessary, from the only recently Prevailed Dark One. He was fully aware that his nature had not been as utterly transformed as his physical body had been by The Prevailation. He understood that his nature had been shaped through many years of torment and abuse and his reactions were still very much as they had been during his captivity. It would take many months of counseling to reshape them.

Aware of the Healer's protective stare, Gairynzvl turned to meet his uniquely viridian gaze and shook his head. "I am not reading you Ayla. You asked me not to and I shall not, but you must then tell me what it is you are thinking. Why are you so confused? Did we not leave Mardan in this state this morning?" The intensity of his purposeful questioning stretched the taut cord between them and she turned away from him once again.

"But I saw him," she muttered, half to him, half to herself. Her thoughts swirled as she tried desperately to return to that moment when they stood in the Chamber of Radiance; when he had drawn her so close to him and she had felt the potency of his emotions as well as the sting of envy radiating from the chamber doorway. She recalled opening her eyes and catching sight of Mardan's cerulean gaze watching them covetously, but if it had been him why was he now asleep, adrift as he had been when the day started? She closed her eyes tightly, trying to pull some clue from the brief seconds when she had seen him that might unravel the mystery.

"You saw him? Where?"

She sighed once again, as if in defeat, and turned back to Gairynzvl. Stepping closer without speaking, she reached out to take his hands and looked down at them with resignation before lifting her gaze to smile wanly up at him. "You are right. It is much easier this way."

He returned her gaze, confused by her circular emotions and logic. In spite of her efforts to dissuade him from doing so, she whispered reassuringly through her thoughts. "Go ahead, it is all right. I cannot explain adequately."

Turning his head slowly to the side once more, his expression grew fleetingly suspicious. The years of needing to be ever vigilant against deception were difficult to overcome, but when her gaze did not falter and the steadiness of her hands in his did not quaver, he relaxed and opened his mind to hers. The soft noise of the room around them and the serenading birdsong greeting the new day from beyond the Temple windows faded. He closed his eyes with contentment as the familiar beat of her heart filled his thoughts; as the steady hum of her delicate aura began to vibrate synchronously with his and the soft sound of her voice returned into his consciousness. The intimate contact was as intoxicating as the finest wine and both swayed subtly as they closed their eyes together and communicated without the need for words or rationale. Beside them, the Healer watched, mutely fascinated.

The Chamber of Radiance filled his mind's eye. The sting of pain from the purging Light returned through her remembrance and he groaned even as the sound of his own voice echoed in his mind. *"Will you help me, Ayla? Will you help them?"* He felt her apprehension. He saw her mouth fall agape as her mind spiraled in a myriad directions. Uncertainty, as well as motivation, shot through her and, as a result, through him. Even as she considered her answer to his unanticipated question, her gaze shifted to a silhouette outlined in the doorway leading into the Chamber of Radiance. Gairynzvl could not help turning his head as if to see better and more clearly who it was that she saw. Together, they could see the clear, crystalline, cerulean gaze she had seen in the shadows. Together they felt the bitter sting of resentment emanating from that gaze and, although they gazed long upon the memory, neither could ascertain the watcher's true identity.

"Is this Mardan?" he asked out loud, breaking the bewitching spell of their telepathy unexpectedly. Ayla opened her eyes to gaze up at him breathlessly and shook her head. How could it be?

Chapter Two

Brilliant sunshine streamed in through the Nursing Ward windows, washing over Gairynzvl in its fullest measure. All the shutters nearest to his bed had been angled to direct the warming ribbons of light over him. Encouraged to rest throughout the remainder of the morning, not only to regain his strength from the demands The Prevailation had put upon him, but also to prepare both physically and mentally for the celebration the temple inhabitants had arranged for that evening, he had willingly returned to his bed. He resisted the notion of being put on any sort of display and was entirely in opposition to meeting and greeting all the villagers of Hwyndarin who had heard the tale of the young Fey who had fought and defeated a Legion of The Reviled, but Veryth assured him that it was all part of the process of Reclamation. Thus, both weary and resigned, he had closed his eyes in the hope of capturing a few moments of sleep.

Lying beneath the radiance of sunlight for the first time in his adult life, Gairynzvl sighed profoundly more than once. The sensation of warmth washing over him was sweetly intoxicating, like the euphoria that spreads through the body after drinking a strong brandy or robust wine,. He did not feel the spreading warmth within, but on his skin and could not keep himself from checking again and again in order to assure himself that the light was not, in any way, burning him. He had become so accustomed to shielding himself from any light that forcing himself to lie within its full and ruddy glow was almost terrifying. Fearful of falling asleep amidst the lustrous gleam lest he not awaken, he tossed and turned for the better part of an hour, but he could not resist the blissful tranquility of the warm sunlight any more than he could deny his exhaustion. Before the chiming bells that heralded the hours rang out from one of the many Temple towers, sleep stole forward in the hazy blush of light caressing him and subdued his anxiety.

* * *

With both friends now a-slumber, Ayla was left on her own. She paced the length and breadth of the Nursing Ward uneasily, turning the memory of cerulean eyes and covetous emotion over and over in her mind. It made no sense to her. Mardan had stood gazing upon them from the shadows behind the doors to the Chamber of Radiance, but now he lay drifting as he had done for days. How had he arisen from his bed unaided and unnoticed? How had he known where to find them and how had he wandered the vast corridors and avenues of the Temple complex, which stood between the Nursing Ward and the chamber where the Prevailation had been performed, without anyone seeing him? Shaking her head, she returned to his bedside and stared down at him, perplexed. His quiet state left her with no answers, only additional questions, but after watching him for many long moments she finally sighed sharply and turned away.

While the malefey slept, Ayla was joined by a companion she knew far better who did not confuse her thoughts or leave her senses spinning. Nayina had arrived with dresses and implements of preparation so they might spend the afternoon in a far more pleasing manner than waiting, alone, in the stillness of the Healing Ward. Having been informed about the celebration planned for that evening by Veryth, who had sent the first invitation directly to her home, Nayina insisted Ayla join her in the rooms that had been provided within the dormitories of the Temple so they might bathe and preen for the upcoming night of revelry. It did not take a great deal of convincing on her part before Ayla agreed to leave behind the confusion prompted by the malefey.

The broad room in which they eventually found themselves was located on the third floor of the Temple dormitories and was warmed by an enormous hearth that stood open on both sides and efficiently heated two rooms rather than one. The room into which they initially entered was a wide chamber with comfortable furniture, several dressing tables with highly polished golden mirrors, which could not be crossed by any Reviled, and a balcony that allowed the afternoon sunlight to stream radiantly into the room. The second was a smaller bathing chamber. It was heated generously by the fire emanating from the hearth and insulated by elaborately decorated tiles that lines the walls and formed intricate, colourful patterns. A large copper bathing tub was situated close enough to the massive hearth that its ruddy heat effectively warmed the water it contained to keep it temperate and inviting.

The afternoon hours passed rapidly. Compelled by Nayina's insistence that she recount of every detail of the Prevailation, a rite she had never even heard of until Veryth mentioned it the previous day, Ayla spent much of the day talking. Athough she did her best to explain what happened, she did not understand most of the elaborate ritual, which made clarifications difficult the many times Nayina stopped her with a query. Nonetheless, the heart of the matter was far less difficult to relate. Gairynzvl had somehow been transformed from a fearsome, dragon-winged, spine-bearing Dark Fey and was restored as a Fey of the Light.

As her thoughts returned to the events of the morning, Ayla's mind filled with the intense emotion she had witnessed and felt, in spite of closing herself to telepathy. The sensations had been inescapable and one did not need to be empathic to sense Gairynzvl's torment or to understand how greatly he suffered during the rite, suffering which prompted tears from her even now. Watching her closely for a quiet moment as she listened intently to her friend's recounting, Nayina posed an unexpectedly piercing question.

"Are you in love with him, Ay?" Lifting her gaze from the depths of the fire into which she had been staring, Ayla looked at her friend and was transfixed with amazement. She tried to instantly deny the fact, but she could not force the negation past her lips. Stammering ineffectually, she could only shake her head with an expression of puzzlement.

"Honestly, Nay, I do not know. How could I be? I have only known him a few days." The questions were meant as much for her friend as for herself, but Nayina shook her head.

"You have known him much longer than just a few days. Isn't he the one who was following you all these past months?"

Ayla nodded mutely, her thoughts whirling as her friend continued.

"I think you were getting to know him all that time without realizing it, just as he was getting to know you."

"It is not as though we ever held a conversation, Nay. How could we get to know each other without speaking?" She was musing aloud, not entirely convinced of the truth her friend was gently asserting, but her companion laughed abruptly.

"You get to know everyone without speaking, Ay. It is, after all, what you do best." The irony of her words brought a smile to Ayla's lips as well. "Perhaps he knew that. Perhaps that is why he lingered close to you for so long. A little underhanded, really, but what do you expect from a Dark Fey?" Her seemingly harmless slur brought a sharp end to her Ayla's musings.

"He's a Dark One no longer, Nay!"

Raising her hands in a placating gesture, the raven-haired shefey quickly apologized. "Forgive me, I am sorry, but all I can see are those fearsome dragon wings and enormous spines of his." Her explanation was emphasized by an abrupt shudder. "Surely they terrify you as much as they do the rest of us, Ay?"

Ayla shook her head, pausing from rubbing oils and botanicals into the lengths of her curling tresses. "He has them no longer; he has been transformed, I told you that."

Nayina stopped and looked at her friend more quizzically, a wrinkle of confusion furrowing her brow. "I thought you were talking about being spiritually transformed; emotionally, mentally. Do you mean to say he was physically altered somehow?" The skepticism of her tone spoke volumes.

"I am not sure how altered he is spiritually. There is so much about The Prevailation I still do not understand, but, Nay, he is not the same as he was yesterday. When you see him tonight you will understand."

Accepting the truth of her friend's statement, Nayina queried no further, though a myriad of further questions filled her mind. Instead, she contented herself beside the warm fire and combed through her hair repeatedly to straighten and dry it as their conversation drifted to less confusing topics. A celebration feast at the Temple was not something that happened every day and the possibilities of the night's festivities spawned more than a few imaginings.

* * *

The liquescently harmonious sound of evening vespers echoed throughout the temple complex, whispering serenely into Gairynzvl's sleeping mind and drawing him back into reality from the lush environs of sleep into which he had fallen. Unaccustomed to waking peacefully, his eyes shot open the moment consciousness returned and he immediately raised himself upward, leaning back upon the heels of his hands as he scanned the room rapidly, searching for any hint of danger or any threat bound to do him harm. Only the soft whispers of the two attendant Healers broke the tranquility. Candles had been lit against the spreading dark of eventide and the streaming sunlight that had soothed and intoxicated him earlier was rapidly diminishing, but even on the brink of nighttide the Temple halls stood tranquil and calm.

He had forgotten. Forgotten where he was and why; forgotten the sensation of security he felt within the ancient halls of the Temple, but as the wisps of cloudy sleep scattered from his mind the hammering of his heart slowed. Shaking his head, he lay back against the warm pillows and sighed prodigiously, closing his eyes while attempting to assimilate the concept of shelter and well-being.

His reverie was short-lived.

Out of the shadows, a figure moved toward him soundlessly like a ghost drifting upon the silent air. It moved past the Healers entirely undetected and stopped beside his bed, pausing to consider him. Wordlessly it waited to be noticed, but he did not immediately open his eyes. Yawning with a greater appreciation of the soothing stillness around him, he almost resented having to rise to face an impending party where he would be the center of everyone's attention and curiosity. Weary in spirit as well as in body, although he had spent the better portion of the day sleeping, he allowed himself the luxury of a leisurely stretch before opening his eyes once again in preparation of rising.

Brilliant cerulean met his gaze, staring at him from out of darkness, but only for an instant before the haze of shadow and blurred perception that shimmered before him shrank back into the dimness of the corridor. Utterly confounded, Gairynzvl sat up and stared into the empty air around him and peered into all corners of the Healing Ward. Unsure if what he had seen was real or the fleeting memory of his earlier joining with Ayla's twisting and chaotic thoughts, which often left him feeling unsettled, he did not wonder about the phenomenon overlong. Even at that moment Veryth was crossing the ward, coming towards him with a broad, welcoming smile and carrying over his arm a set of fresh clothes.

"Valysscopta!" Veryth said cheerfully, then, at Gairynzvl's entirely muddled expression he repeated his greeting in the common tongue. "Fair greetings, friend! I forget that your Celebrae is limited."

Smiling with greater understanding, Gairynzvl nodded and muttered a greeting as well, clearly unaccustomed to the pleasantries of salutations. Veryth's smile never wavered. "I have brought something for you, but we must not tarry here. A room of preparation has been set aside for you and the hour has come to do just that."

Standing In Shadows

Rising hesitantly from his bed at last, Gairynzvl followed the cheerful Healer beyond the ward into the dormitories of the temple, leaving behind Mardan, who still lay unconscious, as well as the mystery of cerulean gazes peering from the shadows.

Chapter Three

Under the protection of dozens of lighted torches that lined the main thoroughfare leading to The Temple, a steady stream of villagers soon began to approach from the forest depths where they made their homes. Responding to hand delivered invitations to dine and celebrate with the Healers, Temple Guardians and The Elders themselves, villagers of all ages crossed the growing darkness of night. Such a summons was not to be ignored, regardless of the thick darkness and brisk temperatures of early winter, and nearly every villager of Hwyndarin turned out in their finest regalia for the event. Progressing with unconcealed curiosity along the brightly lighted way as the pale winter sun slipped beyond the sill of the world, Fey gathered from all directions. A crisp evening breeze swept over the congregation, hastening their otherwise leisurely pace towards the warmth and glimmering crystalline light of The Temple.

The immense complex was off limits to all but the most select or to those who came to the ancient halls to increase their spiritual understanding or physical health, yet most inhabitants of Hwyndarin had never stepped within the glimmering, golden portals and many would spend their entire lifespan without ever glimpsing the sanctuary, Healing Wards or schools of learning inside the surrounding fortified walls. Now, as the extended family of The Fey of the Light drew together and filed through the massive gates in couplets and triplets, a palpable hush descended. Above them, from towering spires and parapets, a bright, clear, exuberant fanfare of horns rang out to welcome all and the peals echoed into the gathering darkness as if to chase it back into the forest depths by the sheer joy of its harmonious sounds.

As the crowds of curious Fey gathered into the Temple they were ushered by hovering guides into a vast chamber encircled by immense pillars of marble and gold. Shielded from the gales of winter by broad windows of multicolored glass, this chamber housed an ensemble of musicians who were awaiting their arrival upon a small dais in one corner of the room before they began playing. Large flutes intricately carved of dark woods, silken-stringed lutes that sang as the sweetest birds, large drums and handheld circles of shimmering bells accompanied two players of the magical, mystical Hudarin. An instrument created by and for The Fey of the Light, the Hudarin reflected in musical tones the mood and emotion of the musician, who, through a great deal of practice, could learn to control the music it created and even direct its sounds.

As the festively decorated hall filled with the sounds of this ethereal music, neighbors and friends found seats at long tables, or milled about in small groups, or stood in doorways speaking about the wonders around them, or watched the musicians playing, or strolled about the chamber marveling at the artistry and workmanship of the architecture and stone work. All awaited the mystery of what the night held in store and each of them had an opinion about what would be revealed.

Away from the gathering crowd in the Chamber of Jollity, Gairynzvl enjoyed the liberty of a hot bath and the opportunity to change his clothes. Dressing in those Veryth had left for him, which seemed to have been tailored to fit him perfectly, he stood before a mirror inspecting his unfamiliar reflection while a male attendant laced the garments round his wings. When the attendant finished this solitary task and had departed, a soft knock sounded upon the chamber door. Starting backwards, Gairynzvl prepared to defend himself, his wings flexing mightily as he tested their strength, but no oppressor or diabolical demon burst into the room intent upon doing him harm and, after a moment, he let out a sharp hiss of breath in exasperation with himself. The soft knock came again, this time slightly more urgently, and he stepped closer to the portal and reached for the handle as, inwardly, he admonished himself for fearing what he knew was impossible. He was within the halls of The Temple, what could possibly happen to harm him?

"Gairynzvl?" A soft feminine voice spoke on the opposite side of the door. It was a voice so unlike Ayla's that he froze once again. His thoughts spun frantically. "Are you there?" The voice queried further; a voice familiar to his ears, yet muffled so that he could not ascertain the speaker's identity. Swiftly, he reached for the handle, twisting it and jerking the door open as abruptly as he could manage, but only an empty corridor greeted him. Puzzled, he stepped out into the dimly lighted passageway, his lavender-ice gaze piercing the darkness and his sharp hearing acutely seeking the slightest sound of retreating footsteps or wing beats, but nothing could be seen or heard in the empty hallway other than the soft sputter of torchlight.

Twisting about, he gazed back into the brightly lit room, seeking shadows that lurked in corners, but there were none and the soft voice he had heard entirely vanished. He stood transfixed, his thoughts twisting with memories as he sought to summon the face of the speaker in his mind's eye, but before he was successful he could hear footsteps coming towards him from the far end of the hall. Refocusing his gaze in that direction, he broadened his stance and drew his wings back in preparation for attack, but he soon let his stance relax as he heard the echo of Ayla's most pleasing laughter. Watching as she came down the corridor accompanied by Nayina, both walking and fanning their wings with blithe contentment, he smiled and shook his head.

Upon seeing him waiting for them in the middle of the passage, their light banter grew quiet and Nayina could not contain an astonished gasp at the sight of him. Uncertain who the tall, strikingly-winged stranger might be, she turned to her friend with a questioning gaze, but Ayla smiled and exclaimed in admiration. "O Gairynzvl!"

Not the same voice he had heard a moment ago. Not the same voice at all.

Stopping several yards away, they stared at him with unguarded appreciation, surprised not only by his remarkable physical transformation, but also that the Temple tailors would ever create an outfit such as the one he now wore. It seemed wholly suited to a Dark Fey. The artisans who tailored and sewed for the Temple inhabitant had well-renowned skill and not without good reason. Their gifts for tailoring lay not only with the use of the finest cloths and the utilization of immaculate stitchery, but with fashioning clothing to the individual that reflected the Fey in both body and in spirit.

The ensemble he wore was as flattering as his own had been, but was made of leather, suede and silken cloth. Black boots came up to the knee over black, leather pants, which had thin vertical stripes of silvery-white stitching. The markings and snug-fitting cut accentuated the strong shape of his legs as well as his striking stature. A tailored vest of black and deep violet suede emphasized the trimness of his waist and his broad chest in the most complimentary manner. Beneath the vest he wore a shirt of silken violet and black and he had folded a full leather coat, trimmed with metalwork, over one arm.

"This is Gairynzvl?" Nayina asked with disbelief, utterly astonished at the alteration he had undergone, but Ayla only nodded mutely, her own thoughts spiraling in a hazy whirlwind at the sight of him. Smiling awkwardly under their combined, admiring stares, he turned aside to extinguish the candles left burning within the chamber he had used and then returned to the hallway where they waited expectantly for him. Even as he stepped out into the hallway once more, Veryth's distinct tenor rang out from the far end of the corridor and the three turned to watch his winged approach. "Valysscopta!"

Bowing formally to him, a senior Temple Healer and Confidant of the Elders, they smiled and stammered the same word in reply, although only Gairynzvl understood the meaning of the Celebrae he used. He returned the greeting more warmly than he had previously and smiled when the Healer alighted near them.

"The hour has come. Jocyndrae Vite! Let us be Festive." In spite of the fact that Veryth made this announcement cheerfully, the newly transformed Dark One beside him could not restrain a grimace at the prospect of celebrating with Fey he could have, on more than one occasion, been forced to cruelly abuse. His misgivings were easily ascertainable through his less than enthusiastic body language and fierce scowl and Veryth gazed at him thoughtfully. "It *is* right to celebrate, Gairynzvl. Do you not rejoice at being set free from the captivity you endured?"

"Of course I do. You know I do." Gairynzvl paused, a pained expression overshadowing his handsome features. "But how can I look into the faces of those gathering below and say 'Jocyndrae Vite' knowing what I have done?"

Veryth's expression did not falter as he listened. Instead, he merely nodded as if he already knew what Gairynzvl would say before he questioned further. "And what is it that you have done?" his tone was measured and calm, but Gairynzvl shook his head with increasing irritation.

"You know very well, Veryth! I have done what all Dark Fey do when they cross into the boundaries of Hwyndarin." Listening to this exchange from a few feet away, Ayla and Nayina drew instinctively closer together, sensing the recently prevailed Dark One's agitation even from their distance.

"I know what the ancient texts tell us, the cruelties we are warned The Reviled visit upon younglings and youthful Fey, but I do not know what *you* have done, Gairynzvl." The Healer's tone remained soothing, almost serene, but his statement also seemed intentionally obtuse. Gairynzvl considered for a moment, his eyes closing as memories engulfed him before he shook his head and retorted brusquely.

"I will not name such vile acts as I was forced to commit."

"Forced?" Veryth queried, his persistently even tone exasperating Gairynzvl further. Stepping closer to the fair Healer, his demeanor suddenly darkened, growing as threatening and confrontational as it had been the night when he had first appeared to Ayla and as it had been when he and Mardan had repeatedly quarreled. Hurling the coat he carried onto the floor at their feet, he hissed at the Healer angrily.

"Yes, Veryth, I was forced. Is that so difficult to believe?" His voice shook with barely contained ire and Nayina could not restrain the gasp of fear that escaped her at witnessing his abrupt shift in temperament any more than she could keep herself from grasping onto her friend and hiding behind her in fear.

Veryth stood calmly and shook his head. "And does not force create a victim?"

Staring back at the Healer while horrific memories shattered through his thoughts like shards of ice, Gairynzvl began to shake with restraint. Veryth continued more insistently. "Is this not what The Reviled do? They force; they coerce; they impose their own despicable will upon another, leaving despair and ruination behind them."

Coming to within inches of the Healer in a rush of unmanageable frustration and violent wing beats, Gairynzvl hissed furiously. "I was a part of that ruination, Veryth! Don't you understand? *I* forced! *I* coerced! *I* imposed! *I* cruelly held another down while the Legion took their pleasure! *I* opened portals so many could defile one! *I* took by force what was not freely offered!" His voice broke as he recounted his crimes, unable to speak further details as the recollections of such harrowing acts visibly ravaged him. Silence stretched taut in the shifting light of the corridor while he paced like a caged animal, gasping for breath before he stammered on in a greater effort to explain himself. "How...how can I look into the eyes of another?...Someone I may have treated so *abominably*...and...and expect them to say Jocyndrae Vite?"

Piercing him with the deep jade of his gaze, Veryth placed his hands upon the young Fey's shoulders, gently drawing him away from the shefey who were plainly distressed by Gairynzvl's appalling confessions. "You were forced to undertake these actions?"

Gairynzvl raised his hands to cover his face in a vain attempt to block the torment of his own memory and contain the powerful deluge of emotion threatening to undo him. Unable to speak further in the fear of wailing out loud or cursing more foully than a DemonFey, he nodded beneath the pressure of the Healer's hands and attempted to turn away, but Veryth held him and spoke more firmly. "Then I say you are a victim as much as those upon whom you were forced to commit these acts. *This* is the Darkness the Reviled wield; the inescapable bleakness that claims the heart and mind and spirit. You, Gairynzvl, may have harmed others while you endured under the domination of Demons. I do not deny that you did, but you were forced, coerced and imposed upon just as cruelly as those you harmed and you suffer an equal torment as they do."

Shaking with barely controlled emotion, Gairynzvl shook his head repeatedly, comprehending the Healer's words but wholly incapable of accepting them. Moved by the influence of his emotion, Ayla endeavored to escape Nayina's grasp and offer some measure of comfort to him, but even as she strove to fend off her friends restraining hands, Veryth glanced at her. Shaking his head with a firmness of gaze that warned her to come no nearer in spite of her sympathetic nature.

"Any one of us, when facing the dreadful consequences you were threatened with if you disobeyed, would choose survival. Anyone would choose to undertake almost any action rather than suffer unspeakable torture and torment. I do not blame you for making such a choice. The Elders do not blame you, Gairynzvl. No one here blames you." Veryth spoke the truth, but unable to contain the emotion pummeling through him, he knocked Veryth's gentle hands away and stepped past him into the guttering torchlight at the opposite end of the hall. Fully aware that the Healer followed him, he desperately tried to escape the searing light of Truth he continued to speak.

"I became a Healer of the Temple to assist those who suffer, whether from illness, grief, or the very great despair caused by The Reviled and I have seen much sorrow and pain in the eyes of others. It is a powerful storm like those that shake the forest in the breadth of summer, but all storms come to an end, Gairynzvl. Do not the ancient texts tell us: '*The shimmer of bejeweled Light ever returns after the storm, transforming what was dark and fearsome into beauty and serenity once again.*'?"

Lowering his hands, Gairynzvl's lavender-ice gaze locked with penetrating jade and he shook his head. "I would not know what the ancient texts tell us."

Undeterred, Veryth continued in a more encouraging tone. "Look around you, Gairynzvl. See where you are. Here, among friends, yet, you stand in shadows. It is your choice what you undertake next. No one here shall force you. None shall coerce you."

Gairynzvl gazed back at Veryth who stood in the glimmering light just on the other side of the shadow that descended upon the far end of the hall where the sputtering torchlight was failing. Darkness had surrounded him, as it had before he had undergone The Prevailation, and he looked outward into the glimmer of the Light with tears upon his cheeks.

"You must choose: either to remain a captive to your anguish and remorse and, thereby, gain nothing for all you have risked, or to lay it aside, like a cloak you remove when you come in from a storm. Your freedom, Gairynzvl, as well as the freedom of those whom you long to help, lies in the choice you make."

Chapter Four

The Chamber of Jollity sparkled in the light of the many candles, torches and frosted lanterns of colored glass scattered throughout the hall. Reflections shimmered from the polished marble floors and the many golden statues and tablets containing ancient inscriptions that lined the hall. Amidst this dancing light, the Fey of Hwyndarin sat at long tables that were laden with baskets of breads and succulent Autumn fruits, platters of steaming vegetables fresh-picked from winter gardens, crockery filled with hearty grains and energizing seeds cooked to perfection with dried fruits and nuts, goblets of fortifying wine and flagons of honey-mead, and fragrant herbs and oils to compliment all. Laughter and music cascaded and echoed through the circular chamber like the tumbling, splashing waters of Veryn Falls and the chattering of Fey, like swarms of contented bees, hummed unceasingly.

Into this bright mirth and hearty communion Veryth strode, the hood of his creamy-white robe pulled back and his smile gracious when Fey who sat near the doorway through which he entered turned to watch him curiously. He was followed, at some length, by Gairynzvl whose own expression was far less amiable and welcoming than the Healer's. At his appearance even more Fey paused from their merriment to gaze curiously at the unrecognized Fey following the Healer into the hall. This attention, however, only made him scowl even more fiercely and he looked downward in an attempt to conceal his discomfort as he followed Veryth to a centrally located platform set to one side of the large table where the Elders, as well as Ayla, Nayina and her companion Reydan, were seated.

The busy hum of chatter diminished to a secretive murmur when Veryth stepped up onto the podium. He waited quietly with an expectant expression brightening his features for the silence that inevitably fell. When it did, he offered the assembly a welcoming smile and raised his hands upward and outward in a sweeping gesture of greeting. "My fellow Hwyndari! Fair greetings. Valysscopta!" His voice rang out enthusiastically and was echoed by a host of cheerful Fey repeating the High Celebrae salutation, whether or not they fully understood its meaning. At the joyful sound, Gairynzvl looked up from the floor beneath his boots and gazed round him in surprise. The bolstering sensation, which the sound of their joined voices had over his spirit, was entirely unexpected. Turning his head, he glanced over his shoulder towards the place at the table where Ayla watched and waited, attempting to whisper to her through his thoughts, but the sound of hundreds of Fey voices drowned out his unspoken words.

Veryth continued with a vibrant, animated tone, "It is with a glad heart that I greet you and offer the hospitality of The Temple Healers, Guardians and, most especially, The Elders, to brighten this darkening hour. We are happy to share this evening of revelry with you, though many among you may wonder at the cause for such an invitation." While he spoke, many Fey paused from eating and drinking, placed their cups down upon their tables and turned to listen more attentively, but there were some among them who were far more distracted by the silent stranger waiting beside the well-known and highly-respected Healer's side. These preoccupied Fey barely heard his words.

"We have called you together this night to share glad tidings and to introduce one who was stolen from our midst at far too young an age." Veryth turned to gaze at Gairynzvl, directing their attention to him as well, and he could not keep from shifting uncomfortably beneath the weight of their combined stares. "We of The Temple know you, my fellow Hwyndari. We know you are a kind-spirited and welcoming people, not quick to judge or malign another. It is our hope and the hope of The Elders that you would give good hearing now to what I have to say." At Veryth's mention of The Elders, those three highly revered Fey quietly stood from their places at the head table and moved upon the wing with barely a sound to alight beside the young stranger. The ethereal radiance of their collective auras brightened the shimmering silver-white of his distinctive wings and hair so that some who watched and listened gasped in amazement or raised a hand to their mouths in wonder.

Veryth's declaration grew more portentous. "Stolen from his home at the age of seven, this young Fey has suffered the cruelty of The Reviled and the unspeakable misery of The Integration for more than fifteen years, enduring with a tenacity of hope that could not be broken." These words brought even greater gasps of astonishment from the assembled Fey as a quiet murmur of uncertainty whispered around the hall. Expecting as much, Veryth continued with greater emotion. "I cannot describe to you, my brothers and sisters of The Light, the torment, anguish, and harsh realities of those years, which he bore alone. I *can* speak, however, of the immense courage and resolute determination required to escape such harrowing captivity."

Gairynzvl ducked his head as he fought back the bitter memories prompted by Veryth's words. The intensity of the Healer's tone began to increase, rising in a measured crescendo that lifted the hearts and spirits of all who heard him. "This young Fey defeated an entire legion of Dark Ones seeking retribution for his defection. He protected a childling and his guardian by closing a portal of crossing rather than opening it, and he nearly sacrificed his life to defend the one of your own young Celebrants. He did all this simply for the chance to escape his captivity." Veryth paused and looked around the room in the heavy silence that had fallen, his gaze connecting with many before he spoke again. "Having been questioned by The Elders and found true in heart and mind to the Light, he has been returned through the Rite of Prevailation to this place, his home; to you, the commune of his family; and to The Light, which is his and our heritage." As he spoke, Veryth moved closer and closer to Gairynzvl until he stood beside him. In that moment, with a Temple Healer at his right side and The Elders at his left, the newly Prevailed Fey was surrounded in the shimmering manifestation of their conjoined aura so that his own, in response to such powerful energy, burned in a bright glimmer of icy-lavender.

"We of The Temple ask now, this night, that you temper your opinions until you may know him better; that you open your arms and wings to him in welcome and that you share this night of feasting and revelry with him in celebration of his return to all that was so cruelly stolen away from him. Therefore, dear Hwyndari, brothers and sisters of Light, friends, family, I introduce to you Gairynzvl and I say to you all: Jocyndrae Vite! Let us be festive!"

A jubilant cheer burst forth from the assembly, startling Gairynzvl so that he stepped back in surprise, his eyes growing wide with amazement, but Veryth smiled broadly beside him. Clasping him about the shoulder in a sideward embrace, he laughed heartily and Gairynzvl could not restrain an uncertain smile in response. Some in the assembly whistled and shouted friendly greetings;

some rubbed their wings together briskly to create deep trills and vibrant trebles of sound that reverberated throughout the hall; some raised their chalices and flagons to him before drinking while others stood and came forward, their hands outstretched to take his and their smiles welcoming.

Although his first inclination was to back away from their zealous reception, his retreat was gently inhibited by the Healer at his side. Smiling with an undeniable expression of hesitation, he stood his ground and accepted their zealous welcome, nodding and muttering words of thanks as skillfully as his severely limited social talents might allow. After several moments, The Elders silently took to wing once again and returned to the head table, drawing back the hoods of their robes and allowing the bright glimmer of their auras to diminish as they joined in the feast. At this unspoken indication, the musicians recommenced their playing and the entire chamber resounded with mirth.

Watching from her place at the head table, Ayla could not help smiling at Gairynzvl's apparent discomfiture that lent him the most unexpectedly endearing aspect. It was a surprising alteration from the fierce Dark One he had been but a brief week ago. Raising her elbows to rest them upon the table, she leaned her chin upon her folded hands and, stretching out her senses to him, quietly listened to the nervous hammering of his heart. She felt the anxiety of his uncertainty that whispered doubts into his mind and heard the incredulous musings that he managed not to speak and she smiled even more brightly. She understood his discomfort completely. She often felt much the same way when confronted by strangers or large crowds and she did not envy him. It was evident that he was overwhelmed, but it was also clear to her, and perhaps to The Elders who silently watched him as well, that he had learned how to conceal his apprehension, insecurity, and uneasiness. It was probably absolutely necessary among the pitiless Reviled. Such signs of weakness would never have been tolerated and, if discovered, would surely have been exploited to torment and abuse him.

Gairynzvl stood unshaken, though shaking, in the midst of a growing crowd of excited Fey who lined up to take the young stranger's hand, to look into the rare lavender-ice of his eyes, to surreptitiously touch his even more remarkable nebulous wings, or to hear him repeat his most uncommon name. He did not falter, not even once, nor did he step backward in an unconscious attempt to evade them, although inwardly every fiber of his being sought escape. Giddy young shefey smilingly approached and bashfully retreated; curious youthful malefey stepped up to greet him while they inspected him from head to toe to wingtip in an unspoken accounting of his attributes with which they might need to compete. Several unified couples welcomed him pleasantly while cloistering their babes and younglings behind them. Even a few oldsters wobbled past him with a half-hearted mutter or stood transfixed by the sight of him, but, at last, Veryth returned to his side and interposed himself between the inquisitive throng and the visibly weary young Fey.

Cheerfully he thanked them for welcoming Gairynzvl so graciously. Then he turned and drew him back to the head table so he might partake of his waiting meal and enjoy some measure of respite. Sitting down beside Ayla at last, he met her curious gaze and whispered through his thoughts a great sigh of relief, though he gave no outward sign of his appreciation for the reprieve. Picking up the golden chalice at his place setting, he looked around him for wine and smiled broadly when Veryth, who had taken the chair next to him, raised a sparkling glass ewer and grinned at him questioningly. Filling his chalice with the luscious, crimson wine Gairynzvl turned to Ayla, inquiring without speaking if she should like her cup filled as well and he received an enthusiastic nod in answer.

Raising these chalices to each other, those seated at the head table finally joined in the celebration. In the moment when The Elders drank the entire host of Fey jubilantly cheered while a peal of horns rang out from the inner halls and outer parapets of the Temple with such exuberance that all who heard the ringing sound smiled. Lifting the goblet he held to his lips, Gairynzvl tasted the wine it contained tentatively and discovered with an even broader smile that it's complex, succulent flavor and sweet finish suited him immensely. Pleased, he tilted his head back and emptied it with delight, reaching for the crystalline ewer to refill the vessel before ever placing it down upon the table.

"Careful." A soft voice whispered near him and he turned to gaze at Ayla quizzically, but she and Nayina were engaged in conversation with a young couple who had come to the table to speak with them. Frowning, he glanced about him briefly, seeking the source of the whisper; yet, finding no one standing near who might have spoken he reached for the chalice and drank freely from it another time.

"Careful, greedy," the voice whisperingly accused, the sound emanating from directly behind him. Twisting round in his chair abruptly, his questing gaze once again fell upon empty air, but his odd behavior drew Veryth's attention and The Healer looked at him, puzzled. Gairynzvl shook his head and scoffed at himself, smiling dismissively at the Healer and raising the ewer to refill both their chalices yet again.

Considering the possibility that Ayla had whispered a warning of temperance to him through her thoughts, he turned back to gaze at her more fixedly. She had never spoken to him in such a taunting manner previously, but the unexpected reprimand had, indeed, captured his attention. Watching her attentively, he noticed for the first time that evening that she had chosen to wear her hair down and he could not keep himself from investigating more closely how it fell in soft ringlets and loose spirals over her shoulders and along her back, rather than being pulled upward in a knot of chaotic curls. Its flaxen lengths shimmered in the sparkling light of the hall inviting his touch as did the dress of fair, blushing pink she wore. Its many layers of silken cloth were dappled with glittering crystals that sparkled in the shimmering light of the chamber and it took all his strength not to reach out to caress her.

Sensing his fervent stare, Ayla turned her gaze to him and then shifted to face him as their thoughts mingled wordlessly. The sound of his heartbeat echoed in her mind, the rush of his breath coming faster filled her with shivering expectation and as his gaze lingered over her bare shoulders and the fitted bodice of her dress, she blushed warmly. Leaning nearer to her, he closed his eyes, seeking the touch of her lips with his and she, wholly intoxicated by more than the wine from her chalice, did not turn aside or push him away. There, in front of the entire assembly, before the Temple Healers and The Elders themselves, she allowed him to kiss her and she eturned his affection with all the emotion that stirred in her heart.

"Careful!" The sharp, feminine whisper came again, forcing him to stop abruptly and open his eyes. He stared at her with confusion.

"Why do you keep saying 'careful' like that?" he asked, a tinge of frustration betrayed in his tone, but she shook her head, nonplussed.

"I said nothing."

Frowning, he turned around once again to gaze about him, growing annoyed by the pestering whisper. As he searched the few shadows that lingered in the furthermost corners, Ayla twisted to look uncertainly at Nayina who watched them both with a sobering expression. Neither of them spoke, but when she turned back to Gairynzvl, Ayla felt certain it had been her friend who had interrupted them with her thoughts of caution. She attempted to reassure him of her friend's innocuous intentions, but when he shook his head and sat back in his chair to watch the festivities of The Fey of The Light with an unreadable expression masking his otherwise handsome features, she knew it was neither the time, nor the place, to press the issue.

Chapter Five

For a long while Gairynzvl sat, quietly watching the mild, pleasant revelry of the Hwyndari while recollections of brash carousing, intemperate drinking, vulgar contests and lascivious enticements careened through his thoughts. When Ayla and Nayina got up to join a circle of other young shefey in an intricate dance that started out stately and measured of pace, but grew in its zeal each time it repeated until they whirled and laughed with the gaiety of younglings, he pushed back from the table abruptly. Snatching up the full chalice of wine he had poured, he hastily withdrew to the far corner of the hall.

There he stood amidst the shadows, watching the serene party unfold and listening to the mystical music of the players as he struggled to control the craving spreading inside him. He wanted to finish the chalice of wine he carried so he might seek out another, and then another and another in a profitless endeavor to quell the ache within the center of his being. It stemmed from the many years of torment he had suffered and filled him with an undeniable sensation of being an outsider. The bright mirth and gentle merriment of the Fey of the Light was foreign to him. He had never witnessed such a subdued celebration and he felt entirely out of place.

"You look a bit lost, friend." A cheerful, male voice marked by a distinctive accent that was not native to the Hwyndari drew him back into the reality of the present moment and he shook his head, focusing his attention on the Fey who appeared close to his same age who now stood before him.

"Do I?"

"No offense intended," the young malefey added as a polite afterthought, smiling affably while he turned to survey the festivities of the evening. "Our revelry must seem," he paused, seeking the correctly word, "tame, in comparison t' wha' you are used."

The glare that met this statement encouraged the malefey to elaborate hastily. "Being in th' Temple, under th' watchful gazes o' th' Elders, it makes a Fey… cautious in his merriment." His smile was enough to soothe the irritation Gairynzvl felt at the approach of the unexpected stranger; nonetheless, he stood guarded and merely nodded. The other tried again. "You do no' find th' wine palatable?'

Gairynzvl looked down into the full chalice he held and shook his head. "I find it very palatable, too much so."

The other concurred with a knowing smile and nod. "Temple wine. Best there is." He raised the flagon he held, meant for mead though filled to the top with crimson wine, and drank with a pleased grin turning his lips. "Goes down easy. Sneaks up on you slow, but like as not, if you drink too much, you shall feel as if one o' th' Elder's kicked you in th' 'ead in th' mornin'," he chortled with a heavy brogue as if he knew from experience and Gairynzvl could not resist his infectious wit. Chuckling dryly, he raised his own cup and drank.

"I'm Rehstaed," the other said offhandedly.

"Gairynzvl," he answered, equally unceremoniously. They considered each other for a moment and Gairynzvl could not help wondering over the other's striking, copper-hued hair, violet eyes and bronze shaded wings; all colors he had never seen before. In their mutual silence the musicians struck up another long awaited tune and amidst cheers and sharp peals of laughter a large circle of dancers gathered in the center of the hall.

"Have you ever ridden a tryngalith bareback?" Rehstaed queried without preamble, as if riding one of the monstrous, six legged, hooved and horned tryngalith from the northern countries was the simplest thing in the world. He received a markedly bewildered expression in answer.

"No. Why would you do that?"

Rehstaed shrugged carelessly. "I dunno. Too much Temple wine, perhaps?" he suggested as a crooked grin slowly turned his lips. His wry wit was inescapable and Gairynzvl could not contain a hoarse laugh. He liked him already.

"Ah, but tell me, friend. D' you ever tire o' th' company of beautiful shefey?" His second question was as astonishing as his first and Gairynzvl could only stare at him, perplexed and uncertain how to answer, but he had no need to. Rehstaed answered his own question for him, his tone filled with incredulity.

"No! An' why would you?" He turned his head and smiled knowingly with raised eyebrows in an unmistakable expression that made Gairynzvl laugh even louder than before. He shook his head and they stood quietly for a moment as the unusual Fey drew a long drink from the flagon he carried. Gairynzvl could not help noticing strange scars upon his forearms when he raised his hand to drink, but he did not question him about them.

Having satisfied his thirst, Rehstaed continued. "Like a not, wit' so lovely a shefey at your side, you will never be wantin' for somethin' t'do, but if you ever wanted to do *nothin'*," Rehstaed leaned closer, looking briefly over his shoulder as if to ensure that the aforementioned, beautiful shefey was not close at hand where she might overhear him when he continued. "*Feel* nothin'; *talk about* nothin'; *share* nothin', or if you want to do somethin' pointless an' ridiculous, just for a laugh, I've a cote near Veryn Falls. You come look me up. It'll be a lark."

Gairynzvl smiled while considering his unexpected invitation and drank once again from his chalice, which was rapidly growing empty. "Near Veryn Falls?" he repeated in a confirming tone, to which Rehstaed smirked and nodded.

"Aye an' you will know it straight away, for 'tis nothin' fancy. No elaborate gardens; no flowers bloomin' save those the birds an' beasts planted; no jinglin' wind chimes; no trailin' incense."

Skeptical as to what sort of place could be so barren and yet, seemingly, so appealing, Gairynzvl frowned doubtfully and scoffed. "What *has* it, then?"

His new friend flashed a mischievously crooked grin at him and raised his free hand, palm upward, in an offering sort of gesture. "Plenty of casks o' Temple wine." His words were exemplified by a tone of such ecstasy that Gairynzvl could not quell his amusement. A broad smile turned his lips as mirth swelled inside him and in his delight he spread his wings and rocked them alternately, closed his eyes, tilted his head back and laughed heartily. Rehstaed laughed as well and the sound echoed through the Chamber of Jollity, melding with the music so perfectly that only one Fey turned their head to gaze with astonishment at them. Without another word, Rehstaed nodded and wandered nonchalantly back into the crowd.

Gairynzvl watched him go, the smile that brightened his features feeling as if it were an unfamiliar mask; yet one which felt intoxicatingly comfortable. As he surveyed the Hwyndari, his enlivened gaze found Ayla once again. She had stepped away from her dancing friends and was watching him with an expression of utter enchantment. Without moving any nearer, he queried through the soft whisper of his thoughts what it was she found so appealing and she immediately answered.

"Your laughter." Without pausing, she moved hurriedly closer, finishing her thought out loud when she stood before him, gazing up into his piercing eyes. "I have never heard you laugh before, but I do like it so very much."

Standing near the far end of the table at which The Elders were still seated, he looked down into her upturned face and allowed the fervent thoughts to return that he had entertained while watching her earlier. His lavender-ice gaze darkened and he whispered to her with unspoken words once again. "I like that *dress* so very much."

Closing her eyes under the influence of his intense stare and the rush of his ardent desire flooding over her with the intensity of a full moon's tide, she sighed both audibly and inaudibly and he would have reached to pull her close right there, but in that moment The Elders rose quietly from their places and approached them. "We shall take our leave of you now and retire," the First of the three began matter-of-factly.

"Our presence often inhibits revelry," the Second continued seamlessly.

"And we do not wish to impede the celebration," the Third finished their united thought; the Three speaking separately, yet as if they were one. Gairynzvl stepped back from Ayla and nodded mutely, though she bowed and replied respectfully.

"As you see fitting."

The First nodded austerely before he continued, "on the 'morrow we shall meet with you, Gairynzvl, to discuss your plan. There is a great deal to decide upon."

Gairynzvl nodded eagerly, a surprised smile turning the corners of his mouth, although he tried to contain his enthusiasm.

"And you, AylaYna," the Second continued, gazing fixedly at her, "you shall need to give an answer to the question he asked of you. He has, indeed, been patient in waiting for it."

Turning his head to gaze down at her, Gairynzvl could both see and feel the apprehension that jolted through her at this obligation, but she bowed subtly and agreed that she would. Then the Third once again addressed Gairynzvl. "Enjoy this night of celebration. It is for you."

Smiling awkwardly, he could only nod, uncertain how to answer the youthful Elder, but before he could formulate a reply, the First spoke yet again. "Allow this revelry to hearten and cheer you."

"Drink deep from your cup, young Gairynzvl," the Second smilingly added and his encouragement was echoed by the Third.

"And fill it often."

Utterly amazed by their endorsement of drinking a good deal of wine, he smiled and happily agreed that he would do his best to obey them. With this satisfactory benediction, The Elders quietly took to wing and departed. The festivities did not instantaneously escalate out of control, but it was not very long before additional quantities of Temple wine were introduced by the servers and as this bounteous supply was being made the musicians put away their traditional instruments and each took up their own Hudarin. At this shifting from temperate to more liberated celebrating and from traditional to more youthful music, most of the elderly Fey quietly withdrew, as did many of the families with younglings and toddlefey. Provision was made for all those who wished to remain within the Temple walls for the night. Dormitories were assigned and many were filled, but those who insisted upon returning to their homes were escorted to their doors by two of the Fey Guard in order to ensure their safety.

As the evening hours deepened into night, the musicians undertook playing less ethereal and far more rhythmic music and many youthful Fey found expression through dancing together. Gairynzvl and Ayla returned to the head table where Nayina and her companion, Reydan, were sitting closely, speaking quietly with each other. She sat absently curling a strand of her straight, chestnut hair round her finger, lazily flexing and stretching her diaphanous wings in contentment as she listened to him whispering softly in her ear and was entirely unaware of them until they sat down beside her.

Upon their return to the table, the two malefey were introduced to each other and the four friends shared a celebratory drink. They discussed nothing more important than the remarkable generosity of the Temple Healers, Scholars and Elders to host so elaborate an evening. They remarked on the deliciousness of the food and succulent wine provided, and their incredible good fortune to enjoy music by such skilled players of the Hudarin, which were very few and far between. The conversation was polite, but uninteresting and Gairynzvl's attention repeatedly strayed to the musicians.

Standing In Shadows

Being unfamiliar with the magical Hudarin, Gairynzvl listened with greater fascination when Reydan, who was himself a musician, described the remarkable talent and discipline required to master the exquisitely sensitive instrument. Created by an artisan musician, the Hudarin was as complexly magical as it was straightforwardly simple. It was at first glance little more than a smoothly polished, oval or spherical object. Yet when taken into the hands, it could translate the emotional or mental energy of the musician into music and, through years of practice and training the musician could learn how to create specific tones, sounds, and even how to vocalize through the instrument.

The players who had been engaged to perform at the celebration to reintroduce Gairynzvl were known for their precise control and ability to play detailed arrangements together as a group. Being able to appreciate the music far better after having heard the explanation by Reydan, Gairynzvl sat back in his chair, took his chalice in hand, and listened intently as the players began a new song, focusing his attention to such a degree that the soft conversation the other three faded into muted, indistinct murmurs.

The piece began with deep fluted tones, rich and airy, while a single bass note, resonant and vibrant so that it could be felt within, played unbroken. As the music began, many of the young Fey familiar with these particular players cheered excitedly and Ayla turned to express to him through an eager, breathless thought that this single player who now played was known as Ryydde. He created the entire song himself, though it sounded like ten players. So extraordinarily gifted, he was the best in all of Jyndari and was said to have been born with a Hudarin already in his hands. Comprehending his unique talent, Gairynzvl nodded and bent the tip of his wing over his shoulder in a gesture to silence her ecstatically prattling thoughts so he might hear the music.

Ryydde's voice then came through the instrument in an echoing, rich tenor, singing in the language of the Ancients the sound of his voice was surrounded by the sounds of bells. After this ethereal beginning, a tribal rhythm of drums began with exotic horns lilting above them while still the deep bass note played on. The music pulsed and flowed invitingly. It seduced the listener with complex, intricate melodies, with primal cadences, and Ryydde's haunting voice as he sang repeating choruses of ancient Celebrae. Interspersed amidst all of this were the occasional sounds of stringed harps like those played in far distant lands and bright scales of trilling bells. The song soared expansively, drawing the listener with it into euphoria, then unexpectedly contracted to the sound of exotic horns and the rhythmic, tribal drums once more. The sound was like that of a wing beat upon a drum. As the song grew in crescendo, all these key elements repeated, merging with melodious tenor; growing in intensity, spiraling upward together in complex harmonies. The music intoxicated; it lured and enticed, until at last with Ryydde's voice echoing as if he alone were a choir of Temple Celebrants, the song decreased, the echo of his voice diminished, and the exotic notes of the single horn faded into the quiet of the hall.

In that moment of silence, the youthful Fey erupted into exuberant expressions of delight and appreciation. Gleeful shouts and whistles rang out along with trills and trebles made by wings rubbed enthusiastically together. Laughter and hands waved high saluted Ryydde's exceptional talent and he, being not proud although he had heard such exultations many times before, placed a hand over his heart and smilingly bowed low with wings curled forward in humility.

Ayla turned to seek Gairynzvl's reaction and found him watching her with a dark glimmer in his icy-lavender gaze. Amid the cheering, a new song commenced in the form of one low, long-held, note serenaded by a single, elegant, seductive horn. The deep, resonant note continued unbroken as the song progressed with sensual melodies and syncopated drum beats, the alluring music building, expanding; yet, slowly, unhurriedly. Ryydde's distinctive, deep tenor once again echoed through the Hudarin and was joined by shefey voices, their wordless vocalizations sweetly beguiling.

Placing his chalice down purposefully, Gairynzvl took Ayla's hand in his and got up. The intensity of his gaze capturing hers and drew her inescapably. Taking a few steps away from the table, he pulled her along with him, much as he had done the first night he appeared to her when he had tugged her behind him down her darkened hallway. She sensed only powerful emotion from him and instinctively resisted, unsure what he wanted. Stopping to look back at her, he stepped so close she could feel his warmth as he looked down into her amber gaze fervently. "Come with me, Ayla." His deep voice was a heavy whisper, which she felt upon her skin when he raised her hand to his lips and kissed her palm warmly, lingeringly.

Her eyes fluttered closed in response to his touch as the persuasive music surrounded them and his tempting desire enveloped her senses. The masculinity of his presence, the intensity of his stare, the deepening passion she felt pounding within him were, together, more than she could oppose. Drawing her out of the Chamber of Jollity into the dimly lighted corridor beyond, he sought a secluded corner, pulling her urgently along with him until he came upon a window at the end of the long hallway. There, in the luminous glow of moonlight, he turned around and embraced her with a deep moan, caressing her with the tips of his wings as their thoughts melded in sighs. Running his hands along her arms, he grasped her more firmly, pulling her upward against him while he stared hungrily at her. Then, he lowered his head to kiss her.

Slowly.

Purposefully.

Moving barely an inch, waiting, then moving closer and pausing to wait once again, he listened keenly to the sound of her unsteady breathing and the less discernible hum of her aura as it began to sing. The touch of his lips upon hers sent a shudder through her that made her sigh sharply, as if she had never been kissed before, and she could not keep herself from leaning into his embrace as the ardor of their kiss deepened. Her senses spun uncontrolled, expanding to encompass his as well as her own and, like the rush of the first spring tide, which consumes the shore upon which it is released, she became lost in the flood of their unified sensations.

Breathless and eager, he kissed her passionately, turning slowly round and stepping forward until her back was against the wall below the window. Effortlessly, he lifted her so she could sit upon the deep windowsill, then he moved as closely as the barricade of the wall would permit, allowing his kiss to trail over her cheeks and chin, finding the soft, rushing pulse at her neck where her skin was more sensitive. Enticing and tempting on one side and then the other with subtle bites and teasing touches of his tongue that sent her senses reeling, he moaned when she responded by leaning backward into his cradling arms, tilting her head back so that her hair cascaded over his hands as she sighed in the glimmering moonlight.

Nearly overwhelmed by the intoxicatingly intimate sensations they shared through their mutual telepathic and empathic abilities, which he had never experienced with anyone previously, he allowed his kisses and the warmth of his heavy breaths to caress the supple curve of her exposed shoulders and the enticingly soft swell of her bosom. The hammering of his heart and the echo of her own as well as the thundering desire within him and the sweet temptation of her body became more than he could bear. Sliding his hands upward along her back, he sought the lacings of her dress, keen to undo them, and she, equally overcome by the exquisite melding of their emotions and mingling sensations, had no measure of desire to deny his endeavor.

He drew a deep, shuddering breath as his thoughts spoke wordlessly to her. *Query?*

Her thoughts answered his own. *Spinning*!

Desire!

Sigh!

Moaning deeply, he ventured to unlace the seams of her clothing, quickly becoming frustrated by the delicate material from which the lacings were fashioned so that he was forced to turn her to one side in order to give his full attention to the infuriating strings of corded silk that closed the lovely dress round her wings. His avid passion caused his hands to tremble, inhibiting his actions to such an obstructive degree that he briefly entertained the notion of simply tearing the garment open.

Laughing breathlessly at his difficulty, she attempted to assist him, but, even as she raised her hands an echo of her name resounded along the dim passageway. In the euphoric bliss of the moment, neither of them paid any attention to this voice. She thought it was him whispering to her through his impassioned thoughts and he did not care what he heard; yet, the echo repeated again, and then another time, growing stronger and clearer as the one calling to her drew closer. "Ayla! Ayla! Come Quickly!"

It was Nayina. She knew not only from the sound of her voice, but from the emotion she felt coming from her long-time friend as she came rushing down the hallway toward them. When she neared them and saw what she was interrupting however, she stopped abruptly and turned awkwardly aside, stammering an apology hurriedly.

"Ayla! Ay...OH! Oh I *am* sorry. But Ayla, you must come. Yes, and you too Gairynzvl. It is Mardan! The Healers say he is waking."

Chapter Six

Ayla's passion dissipated and she hastily attempted to jump down from the window where she sat, but Gairynzvl was much slower in responding to this unanticipated announcement. Placing his hands flat upon the cool stone windowsill on either side of her, he slowly turned his head to the side so neither shefey could see his exasperated expression or the irritation he felt. Closing his eyes and sighing profoundly through gritted teeth, he attempted to gather his senses. The intensity of his desire was not as easily suppressed as hers.

"I am sorry, Gairynzvl," Ayla whispered to him in a hushed tone, placing one hand upon his shoulder, but he shook his head with his eyes still closed.

"I will follow you shortly." The heaviness of his tone spoke volumes and she hesitated, unwilling to simply leave him behind, but he looked up at her and urged her to action more impatiently. "Go."

Sensing his mounting ire despite the lingering passion still hammering inside him, she apologized once more before she slipped past him to join Nayina a few yards away. Together they rushed towards the Healing Ward and left him standing alone in the silent moonlight.

Deeply, he drew a few breaths, attempting to clear his mind and calm himself, but the pounding of his heart and the passion rushing within him wrought havoc with his senses with the unruliness of a summer storm. Leaning heavily upon his palms, he lowered his head, closed his eyes once again and tried to concentrate on what should have been fantastic news.

Mardan was waking. After the horrifying beating he had suffered at the hands of the Centurion, he should have been thankful for such a miracle; still, at that precise moment, he could not find it within him to care in the slightest.

Lifting his head to stare blindly at the stone archway above the window, he vented his dissatisfaction and vexation in the only manner available to him.

"Raach!" He cursed loudly, the harsh Dlalth word echoing through the dimly lighted corridors of the Temple incongruously. Silence prevailed. Then a soft sound captured his attention, like that of silk rustling in the evening breeze, Turning his head to the side, he listened more intently.

"She's an insensitive mite."

It was the same shefey voice he had been hearing all day and it came from directly behind him. Turning ever so slightly to one side, he answered the voice warily. "Does it matter to you?"

"Of course it does!" The voice became a whisper in his ear and he could feel the speaker's breath on his cheek, though there was no visual sign of the shefey addressing him. He smiled and queried more cunningly.

"Why should it?" His answer was the unexpected sensation of being touched; a caress that brushed boldly up his thigh and across his hip.

"You know why."

"That is a unique talent," he laughed heavily. "I know of only one with such a gift."

"I should hope so!" The voice answered, then, in a wrinkle of light that beguiled the eye a lovely young Dark Fey appeared beside him out of the darkness.

"Ilys!" he exclaimed in a surprised whisper as he turned round to greet her, his tone betraying his delight as well as his astonishment at seeing her. She smiled with evident satisfaction.

She stood taller than Ayla and was attired audaciously, not in a lovely dress as Ayla often wore, but in fitted black leggings with thick silvery-gray, vertical stripes. She wore black leather boots up to the knee and, although they were fashioned with a small heel, three broad belts of leather wound about her calves, each fastened with a bright silver buckle. Another belt of leather fit snug round her hips, holding a small pouch emblazoned with the abstract design of a dragon. Her shirt of silvery-gray was worn beneath a black leather corset, not laced in the usual manner, but clasped down the center of the garment with metal fastenings that interlocked with each other. Yet, in spite of her nonconformist manner of dressing, her most striking feature was not what she wore at all.

Above her temples, two large, silver horns arched backward over her delicately pointed ears, curling upward and slightly outward as they extended back a full ten inches. Another pair of horns grew immediately below this first set; yet these curled downward around her ears to point forwards, the glimmering tips of which stopped just below her high cheekbones. These horns of metallic sheen were mirrored by sharp spines that extended from the joints of her fearsome, dragon-hide wings, though they were far smaller and less ferocious than Gairynzvl's had been. Her shoulder length, silvery hair was tinted here and there by dark crimson hues and two braids, one on either side of her face, were pulled back and cinched round with a single strip of leather.

"What are you doing here?"

Ignoring his query, she moved closer to him, tracing the v-pattern of his vest that began at his chest and descended to his waist. "I came to see you. Aren't you happy to see me?"

The familiar sensation of her hands upon him ignited memories as well as the lingering embers of his present passion. Closing his eyes, he sighed involuntarily and this was answer enough for her. "She should never have flitted off like that leaving you so unsatisfied." Her tone was full of suggestion and he understood her only too well. Reaching to stop her hands from straying too boldly, he shook his head.

"She had good reason to go and I am not angry with her."

"It didn't sound that way to me," she disagreed coyly, freeing her hands from his to walk round him slowly, inspecting him openly from head to toe to wingtip. "I'm not sure I like this new look on you, 'Rynzvl. Don't you miss the power of your Dlalth wings?"

He scoffed at the way in which she toyed with him and turned to follow her movements. "Perhaps, but you have not answered my question."

Pausing, she looked up at him in surprise. "I had to find you. None knew where you had gone and then, the few Legionnaires sent to bring you back returned with a tale so unimaginable it has sparked full scale preparations."

Alarmed by this unforeseen report, his expression darkened. "Preparations? For what?"

Raising her hand unexpectedly, she slapped him sharply. "For retribution you fool! What did you think would happen when you close a portal on your centurion and then kill him when he comes to reclaim you?"

Grasping her by the wrist, he stepped menacingly closer, glaring into her dark cerulean eyes with a potent combination of anger and unanticipated desire. Flexing his powerful wings aggressively, they stared at each other in tense silence and time seemed to stutter to a halt. His breathing became as heavy as it had been only moments before as he fought to control the torrents of emotion and desire colliding within him. Wrenching her arm sideways, Ilys attempted to free herself, but when she was unsuccessful she half closed her eyes seductively and looked up at him through her lashes.

"I had to warn you," she explained in a soft, inviting whisper.

His thoughts swirled like a maelstrom and before he could set any measure of restraint over his passions she reached upward, entangled her fingers in his hair and pulled him down to kiss him. Unprepared, he stood immobilized by her kiss and the persuasive memories it evoked in him. They had been friends a long while in the harrowing realm of the Uunglarda and had comforted each other in the secret moments they stole together and their friendship had transformed into a far more intimate relationship. He remembered the hours they had surreptitiously shared, hidden from the ever vigilant surveillance of the Centurion by Ilys' extraordinary gift as a Light Bender. These thoughts swam in his mind like the influence of strong wine, reigniting the flame of his denied desire and he could not stand motionless in the blaze.

Wrapping his arms around her in a tight embrace, he pulled her against him as he returned her kiss feverishly, hurriedly recalling the peril of kissing her too enthusiastically when the tips of her horns pressed treacherously into his cheeks. His hands rediscovered the supple curves of her body and the enticements of her atypical manner of dressing. Yet, even while he responded to her physically, the emptiness of the moment, the hollowness of not hearing her inner thoughts or sharing the dizzying swirl of emotion building between them as he and Ayla had done, pierced him like a blade.

Abruptly, he pulled away and stared down into her upturned face as he struggled to comprehend why his thoughts should be filling with Ayla at such an inopportune moment. Confused, Ilys drew him back to her, continuing their kiss while he sought to understand himself. Physically, he wanted nothing more than to lose himself to the moment, their reunification undeniably compelling, but instead he found himself attempting to break free from her yet again.

"Stop." His heavy tone belied his unanticipated request and she ignored him. Raising his hands to her shoulders, he pushed her back more insistently, but she giggled impishly, assuming his actions were meant to tempt her as they had often done before.

"Stop." He repeated in a more imposing tone, seeking to take hold of her hands before her caresses made his actions futile, but she recalled other hours spent with him and smacked his hands playfully. She could not hear his unspoken words as Ayla did; she never could, and her gift of being a Light Bender, of making herself invisible, also gave her the ability to block telepathic senses. This gift had protected her in countless situations by allowing her to go completely unnoticed, but the inability to read her or to express to her through his thoughts that he no longer desired such a relationship from her increased his vexation until he grabbed her by the wrists and shoved her away forcefully. "I said stop! Is this all you can think of? Was there no other reason you undertook so perilous a journey in coming here?"

Astonished and a bit outraged by his refusal, she glared back at him angrily, flexing her wings repeatedly in annoyance. "You never used to be so full of complaints."

He shook his head, stifling the physicality of his need with anger. "I am not what I used to be. That is the point of The Prevailation. I thought you understood that."

Silently she stared at him, unwilling to admit that so much had changed in so short a time; yet, unable to beguile herself into believing it had not. He was indeed different and the alteration was not merely physical. She no longer held his interest as she once had done. Her stare grew aloof, unreadable, although she did not speak a word. Turning aside, she stared out the window into the moonlit night and answered in a far more guarded tone. "Perhaps I was testing you. Perhaps I needed proof that all these miraculous things you've been saying about the Prevailation are true."

Closing his eyes in a greater attempt to settle his raging desires, he raised his hand to cover his face even as he answered. "And now? Will you return to the Uunglarda and tell them what I have done and all I plan to do?"

She scoffed at his query and spun on her heel to face him once more. "They don't need me to spy for them, 'Rynzvl. They already know as much as they need to know about what you have done. As for what it is you plan to do, you already know how I feel about that."

His irritation with her elusiveness mounted, as it ever did when they spoke about anything seriously. "What, then, have you decided to do? Will you remain and help me?"

Silence answered him and her eyes narrowed slightly as she contemplated her reply. "I might have been prepared to assist you, but this alteration," she gestured at him doubtfully, "I cannot see how it can serve you or how it will protect you. You've left yourself vulnerable and weakened."

Hissing in frustration, he moved to within inches of her to glare down into her upturned face, demonstrating for her scrutiny the full measure of strength he still possessed. Stretching out his wings to their fullest extent, nearly fifteen feet from wingtip to wingtip, he directed a current of air at her with one powerfully aggressive motion of wing that carried such force she was pummeled into the wall behind her without his ever needing to touch her. "I am far from weak or vulnerable," he growled.

Gasping, she gathered her balance and righted herself, pushing herself up from the floor below the window and laughing dryly in an attempt to disguise her surprise at his display of hostility. "Oh! There you are, Gairynzvl. I thought I lost you."

He shook his head, tired of her toying, and moved away from her as he strode purposefully in the direction of the Nursing Ward. "I must go. They are waiting for me and my prolonged absence will only raise questions."

"What you plan to do is noble, but do you think the Dlalth will stand idly by and allow you to steal their future from them?" She hurled her words after him, succeeding in capturing his attention another time. Twisting round, he paused to glare back at her quizzically. "They will come with legions upon legions to this realm. They will hunt you down like blaylscith and tear this village apart in the process, killing and doing far worse to as many as they possibly can. You know this."

She spoke the truth and he could not deny it. Staring at her without speaking, he wished with all his heart she had the ability to understand him the way Ayla did; that she could feel the intensity of his emotions. His absolute need to do whatever he could, if even to rescue only one, but his silence did not communicate any of this to her. Placing her hands on her hips, she posed one final question. "Are the lives of a few childfey worth so much?"

Staring back at her incredulously, he nodded unhurriedly. "Hide yourself, Ilys and be wary of Ayla. She is an empath of extraordinary ability and will sense you long before she can see you. Tomorrow I will meet with The Elders to discuss my plans. If you intend to help, remain hidden until the appropriate time. If not, if you intend to return to The Uunglarda and offer a full report, then it is here and now that we say farewell." Then he continued toward the Nursing Ward without looking back.

Chapter Seven

The chimes outside the Healing Ward quietly tolled the hour of one, but those gathered within paid little heed to what time it was. Standing round the bed in which Mardan lay, those friends and Healers who had drawn close waited in tense silence as Ayla laid her hand upon him, closed her eyes and sought for his thoughts. Prepared to seek deeply for them as she had done so often before, she could not contain the startled gasp that escaped her when he reached up unexpectedly to take her hand and her exclamation of surprise was echoed by those around her. Opening her eyes, her tear-filled amber gaze met his of crystalline cerulean and she could not keep herself from instantly leaning down to embrace him.

Such poignant emotion flooded through her, emotion of her own as well as the monumental relief and elation of those standing round, that she did not have the strength to combat the tide. Pressing her face into his chest, she embraced him as tightly as their awkward position might allow and she wept deeply, even as he returned her affection in the only manner his weakened condition permitted, amazed by such a display of sentiment. Wrapping his arms about her, he inclined his head towards hers and closed his eyes, moaning uncomfortably when she pressed too close in spite of how good it felt to hold her.

Ayla gasped aloud, trying with all her might to contain the torrents of emotion surging all around her, although it took many moments before she was entirely successful and could straighten to gaze down at him with a bleary expression. Quietly Nayina stepped behind her, offering a small handkerchief and embracing her friend by the shoulders as she smiled down at Mardan with tears restrained within her eyes as well.

"It is, indeed, a blessing that you have returned to us, Mardan." The attendant Healer with viridian eyes spoke quietly, voicing their shared amazement and delight, but Mardan shook his head in response. Releasing Ayla, he gazed past her at the others curiously.

"Is it? Where have I been?" The softness of his voice betrayed the lingering weakness he still felt, as did the weariness haunting the depths of his gaze.

"You have been far, far away for many days, Mardan," Ayla explained through the swell of emotion assailing her.

"Sleeping deeply as your body tended and healed your injuries and renewed your strength." The Healer added more informatively. Silent, Mardan nodded and closed his eyes for a protracted moment, seeming to have slipped back into sleep without another word. No one moved, nor barely breathed; yet, at length, he opened his eyes once more and looked about him at those watching so attentively. Smiling feebly, his gaze then sought more curiously. "Where is Gairynzvl?"

An uncertain hush met this question, but before any could offer excuses for his absence, the deep voice of their missing friend answered from the doorway. "Here." The newly transformed Dark One strode into the room quietly, uncomfortable at having not been present at such a significant moment while simultaneously uncertain if he deserved to be there at all. As he drew closer Mardan focused his gaze on him with an expression of wonder brightening his features and pushed himself up into a half recumbent position in order to take in the stunning transformation he had undergone.

"The Prevailation has already been performed?" he inquired with a hint of disappointment, clearly wishing to have attended such a rare ceremony, to which Gairynzvl nodded.

"Just this morning." Stopping at the foot of the bed rather than moving to stand beside Ayla, he did not look at her when the awkward confusion of her thoughts sought to touch him. Instead, he allowed Mardan's inquisitive stare to center on him, which, in turn, drew the gazes of the others as well. Shifting awkwardly, he drew his wings closer with instinctive caution, but Mardan shook his head and spoke with amazement.

"Remarkable."

Gairynzvl scoffed doubtfully. "The only truly remarkable one here is you, *Celebrant*," he responded kindly, although the derogatory manner in which he spoke the word 'Celebrant' and the half snarl with which he said it made the

Healer beside him turn his head sharply to stare at him. However, Mardan laughed dryly and smiled.

"I do not presently feel remarkable, *Dark One*," he returned with equal derision, causing the Healer even greater distress, as he feared some quarrel might ensue, but Mardan quickly followed this slight with a smirk and continued more lightheartedly. "Though it would seem I can no longer call you that."

Gairynzvl grinned back at him wryly. "*You* might be the only one who yet may."

"You must tell me all about The Prevailation," Mardan said, his voice filled with curiosity and Gairynzvl would have undertaken to sit down and share his story, but the Healer interjected hastily.

"I would advise against that." The sharpness of his tone caused all those who stood round Mardan's bedside to gaze at him incredulously so that he quickly clarified. "Upon the morrow, Gairynzvl, you can share your tale in the fullest measure, but for now I believe Mardan should rest."

Ayla sighed sharply at this pronouncement, but Mardan nodded, his eyes closing involuntarily even as he did so. "Sage advice, Healer, for although I do wish to hear every detail of your story, *Dark One*, I know I would not stay awake long enough to listen in completeness."

Gairynzvl nodded as well and stepped back from the bed. "Until the morrow, then, *Celebrant*," he returned with equally feigned derision. Then, without speaking another word, he turned and strode towards the door. In that moment Ayla's thoughts swept after him in a torrent of uncertainty, desiring to know where he was going and longing for him to wait while at the same time she was indecisive about her feelings because she also wished to remain with Mardan. Sensing the chaos of her present state of being and not bothering to turn his head or pause in his retreat, Gairynzvl answered the tide of her unspoken questions with a single thought. "*Tomorrow.*" Then he continued through the portal into the dimness of the corridor beyond.

The others who had gathered around him bid Mardan and Ayla a good eventide and retired for the night as well, but Ayla lingered, longing for a moment of privacy during which she could speak more confidentially with her Celebrant friend and lover. After making certain that he had no immediate needs, the Healer also withdrew, leaving them alone at last.

"Will you remain for some while as I sleep?" Mardan asked quietly and she nodded, sitting down upon the edge of the bed though her thoughts followed

Gairynzvl, worrying and wondering after him. "His transformation is amazing," he stated deliberately, capturing her full attention at last. Unable to hide the guilty expression that betrayed her, she stared back at him in flustered silence, but he shook his head. "I have not been with you these past few days, but it is not difficult to see you care for him, Ay."

She stammered hesitantly, truly unable to justify her feelings, but Mardan did not require an explanation. Instead he continued in a tone that was filled with uneasiness. "I would only ask you to remember that the magic of The Prevailation does not alter the person within. That which he is; the person he has learned to be through the harshness of life in the Uunglarda, yet remains."

Ayla nodded, already having sensed the inner turmoil that lingered inside Gairynzvl, but her heart stubbornly refused to listen to reason. Sighing profoundly then, Mardan closed his eyes and muttered in a weary whisper. "I might also ask you to recall all we have shared." With this, he drifted into sleep once again, leaving her watching him amidst a mayhem of musings and emotions that swirled within her like madness. Long she remained beside him, struggling to understand herself; yearning for the return of simpler times when Mardan's affection was more than enough for her and fretting over the dangers of Gairynzvl's plan. At the same time, she understood his desire to help those whom he could not help until now. She knew she would be required to answer his question when they met with The Elders in the morning and this single thought kept sleep from finding her until the very early hours of morning.

* * *

The Elders sat on a marble bench that stood upon a raised dais several steps above the shimmering marble floor of the Temple Devotionary, a room where they spent most of their days. They awaited the arrival of Gairynzvl and Ayla and were silent of speech, although they communicated with each other through the telepathy of their thoughts. Seated in a trance-like state with eyes closed and their combined auras radiating brightly, they shared their concerns about the newly Prevailed Dark One's plan as well as their reservations about sharing what he would be doing with the village because of the inevitable repercussions of his actions. War could come to their tranquil lands, but they each agreed it was a risk well worth taking. It was time to act.

In the sparkling morning sunlight that cascaded through the room in ribbons of incandescent light, joyful birdsong from the forest surrounding the

Temple melded with the harmonious sounds of morning prayers and chanting coming from the sacred Inner Chamber. The Elders sat quietly, their auras gently pulsating, until The Third opened his eyes. Turning his head to look at his brothers, he raised a single brow as a tense presence filled their awareness from just outside.

Outside the Devotionary, in stark contrast to these peaceful musings and lilting tones, Gairynzvl paced the corridor with agitation, his patience all but spent waiting for Ayla to arrive. He did not have to wonder about where she might be; he already knew she had stopped by the Nursing Ward to visit Mardan before joining him for their meeting with The Elders. She surely would be rekindling her feelings for her Celebrant lover, in spite of everything they had just shared only a few hours ago. She surely would not agree to help him in the face of the danger such a proposition proposed. If she truly desired to use her gifts for some purpose of good, would she not have answered him straightaway rather than making him wait? He scoffed out loud and stood for a protracted moment glaring out of the nearby window with his hands resting lightly upon his hips while he gave expression to his frustration through several vehement wing beats. Making him wait was what she seemed to do best. For one brief moment his anger flared. If he had been in the Uunglarda, he would have reached for the nearest object and hurled it against the wall, but the nearest object was an ancient, priceless vase standing on a small pedestal so he contented himself with several additional furious wingbeats.

Hearing the approach of rapid footsteps echoing from the distance, Gairynzvl paused and looked up, seeking the source of the sound and he was not surprised to hear the commotion and disorder of her jumbled thoughts or to see Ayla rushing to meet him after staying overlong at Mardan's bedside. Shaking his head with even greater frustration, he stepped towards her as she came nearer, not bothering to greet her with the customary morning pleasantries before besetting her with his pent up vexation. "Where have you been? What have you been doing? Do you not realize The Elders are waiting for us? Why must you keep me waiting when you know what this means to me?"

She slowed dramatically and stared at him with astonishment at his unexpected reprimand. "I am sorry, Gairynzvl, I was speaking with,"

"Mardan, yes I know."

Arching her wings backward, she stopped in her tracks, crossed her arms over her chest and stared at him with open-mouthed annoyance. "You said you would not read me without my permission," she retorted sharply, but he shook his head, spinning on his heel to take up his pacing once more.

"I do not need to read you, Ayla, to assume where you have been so long when you should have been here."

She hissed at his disdainful reply in an atypical display of irritation and turned aside as well. "I did not intend to be so long. I just wanted to be sure he was all right, but he wanted to speak with me."

Again Gairynzvl interrupted her with an acerbic rebuke, "Trying to convince you not to help me, no doubt."

"Gairynzvl, will you please stop doing that," she snapped and he turned to look at her with an expression that betrayed all of his writhing emotion.

"Mardan could not possibly convince me not to do something he knows nothing about, but why should you be surprised that I am uncertain about agreeing with your plan?"

He hissed and flexed his wings angrily. "If you truly cared for others as you profess to you would not hesitate."

Growing more cross at his irascible behavior, she shook her head. "What is that supposed to mean?"

Having waited so long and suffered disappointment more than once because of her emotional dithering; having felt the lash of the Reviled's whip as well as the scourge of the Prevailation's Light, he sighed sharply. He had little patience left to combat the rising tide of his annoyance with the entire situation and even less practice with diplomacy of any form. Unable to express himself in any other manner, he rounded on her viciously. Moving to within inches of her, he glared down at her as he had done on the first night they met, his lavender-ice stare piercing her as effectively as his crimson glare had done that first, fearsome night. Spreading his wings to their fullest, he held them over her head in a threatening display and growled in answer. "I thought you understood. I thought you felt what I suffered and would never refuse to help those innocent ones who live under that same torment as I did, but you are far too concerned with your own safety and with your own pleasure to think of others."

Appalled by his scathing accusation, she stared back at him mutely, openly aghast, but he did not give her time to collect her thoughts to formulate a rebuke before he continued even more impatiently.

"They are *Childfey* Ayla! Babes and toddlefey who are neglected, abused, and tormented! They suffer ALONE all the pain and anguish you felt through me.

How *can* you hesitate? I thought as a Guardian you were dedicated to protecting the innocent. That is why I came to you. I thought asking for your help would be uncomplicated, but you seem to make *everything* complicated."

Tears rimmed in her amber eyes in spite of her anger, though her emotion was not instigated by his caustic reprimand or as a result of him forcing the memories of his own Integration upon her again. He did not have to; she remembered the horrors of his past well enough. As they stood staring at each other, the broad doors of the Devotionary opened and Veryth gazed out at them, his customary smile diminished at the sight and echoing sounds of their quarrel. Stepping to one side in an unspoken invitation for them to enter, he tucked his hands into the broad ends of his sleeves and lowered his head unobtrusively. Giving them a moment to allow the tempest of emotion writhing between them to calm, he was surprised when Gairynzvl shook his head and turned away from their locked stare first.

The passions roiling within him and his fierce impatience made him bold, in spite of the immense honor a meeting with The Elders represented. Striding purposefully up to the dais where the Three waited silently, he checked himself only when he reached the base of those marble stairs. Stopping awkwardly, he gazed at them curiously before he twisted around to gaze behind him for Ayla. She hesitated, clearly uncertain about the choice she was obliged to make, but Veryth moved beside her and gently ushered her into the chamber. She had heard about the Devotionary many times, but never dared to dream she would ever see it, let alone go inside. The private chamber of reflection and mediation of The Elders was a place no place for common Fey, yet now she was standing before them with a newly Prevailed Dark Fey at her side.

All at once the rush of the Elder's thoughts poured into their minds, like a torrent of echoing sound as inescapable as thunder. The Three spoke as one through the means of pure thought alone and Ayla, being unaccustomed to telepathic communication with the exception of Gairynzvl's soft whispers, grimaced and started backward in surprise. He, however, did not even flinch.

"The hour of decision has come." Their voices seemed to echo in spite of the face that they did not speak a single word. "A desire to help those who cannot help themselves has been expressed and action is appropriate. This is a just and admirable cause, one we Fey of The Light have been unable to undertake before this day; yet the Prophecy of Reclamation seems to have been fulfilled.

The One who walks in Light and Shadow, spoken of in the ancient texts, has come forth and his Purpose shall not be impeded."

What they said was as shocking to her as the manner in which they said it and Ayla stared at them in absolute astonishment, her thoughts scattering in a dozen directions as she sought to recall the precise text they referenced. Even Veryth, who heard their pronouncement as clearly as she and Gairynzvl did, gazed back at them with evident amazement, although his response was tempered with calm serenity as he recited the words of the ancient prophecy.

"*Out of the Darkness, Light shall burst forth, Indomitable. And the Light will Prevail over the Darkness by shining into it, Unwavering; Guiding the Innocent from shadow and the irresolute from placidity.*"

Chapter Eight

In the silence that filled the room after this declaration, the echoing birdsong of morning poured in through the high, half shuttered windows as a litany of music to the long disregarded divination. Outside in the sky, the clouds shifted and brilliant sunlight streamed into the Devotionary in a single radiant stream that shimmering upon Gairynzvl's nebulous wings and through his silvery-white hair as if the ancient authors of those words had planned just such a moment.

The Elders turned by one consent to gaze on this light as it fell upon him, watching the window from where it streamed as if such an unexpected occurrence surprised even them and for one brief moment the light rippled, diminishing for an instant before blazing in full radiance once again. Ayla gasped and stood staring at him, her senses spinning, her hands trembling, and her heart fluttering. Whether this reaction was in response to the amazement she felt or from a deeper, far more zealous emotion, she could not clearly define. Unaware of the light sparkling around him, Gairynzvl stood silently, waiting for The Elders to continue. He waited for them to ask him to explain his plan in detail and for them to require an answer from Ayla, an answer he could not seem to force from her himself, but for many protracted moments they did not speak.

At last, the thunder of their thoughts returned in their minds. "We have felt your anguish, Gairynzvl. We have seen the torment inflicted upon you by The Reviled. We have heard the echoes of your grief, your desolation and your anger," the Elders continued. Unaccustomed to such powerful thoughts, Ayla could not help wavering unsteadily under the powerful influence of their combined telepathy, but Gairynzvl neither moved nor looked away from the brilliance of their conjoined aura or the intensity of the direct channeling of their thoughts. "We know only too well the torture of The Integration and understand, through touching your mind and spirit, how brutal and unrelenting that abuse is in every way. We comprehend your desire to help those younglings who are unable to free themselves from this captivity and we agree the time has come to render any aid we are able to give. Still, there are contingencies to consider; there are preparations to be made and there are questions as yet unanswered."

Looking beyond Gairynzvl, the united gaze of The Elders settled upon Ayla, as it had done many years ago when she was just a child living in the Temple training to become a Guardian of Childfey. All the measures taken those many years ago to focus her abilities, to fortify her knowledge with incantations of protection and magic and to create in her a ministering spirit now seemed to take on a new light and a truer purpose. Closing her eyes, she drew a deep, shuddering breath and attempted to compose her answer, but when the voice of The Elders poured into her mind asking once again what Gairynzvl had already spoken it was not her intellect that answered.

"AylaYna, daughter of AyannaDvnna and Bryndan, you have been dedicated as a Guardian of the Innocent, a Protector of Babes and Younglings. You have been asked to render aid in the rescue of those childfey stolen away by The Reviled and the time of decision is upon you. What answer do you give?"

Trembling from head to toe to wingtip, Ayla opened her eyes and her amber gaze locked with Gairynzvl's lavender-ice stare when he turned to look back at her. In that brief moment, every emotion he had forced upon her on the first night they met flashed through her consciousness. Every memory he shared with her of his harsh and pain filled years of captivity shattered through her thoughts, but most especially his heart wrenching descriptions of the treatment the childfey were forced to bear during The Integration and she found herself nodding even before a single word could form. She was not poetic or lyrical; in truth she had little skill at speaking, but the only word that mattered rushed from her lips as if by its own volition. "Yes."

The amazed expression that overtook him spoke more clearly than any words he might have been able to say, if, at that moment, he could have managed to say them. Instead, he stared at her with bewildered surprise, a smile slowly curving his lips, but before he could move to her or find anything intelligible to say, The Elders continued.

"Will you stand by Gairynzvl, even in the depths of Darkness?"

Again the answer rushed from her as if upon wings. "Yes."

"Will you help him, even in the face of fear, evil, danger?"

Rather than wavering in the light of such considerations, the rush of compelling emotion she felt brought the answer to her lips once again before she could consciously form the word. "Yes."

"Will you share with him your capacity for peace, joy and hope when you find only shadows? Will you comfort him even when there is no comfort to be found?"

"Yes."

The Elders turned to look at each other, nodding in union as if all their efforts, all the hours spent teaching her those many years ago, had suddenly come to fruition. Then their cohesive gaze fell upon Gairynzvl, but their words did not come to him in the rush of pure thought. Comprehending Ayla's taxed mental condition as a result of their powerful method of communication, they chose to continue by speaking verbally, as one; their individual voices amalgamated into one sound. "Gairynzvl, son of Light and Sorrow, you have been given the aid of a true Guardian of Childfey. Her strength is her weakness. Her powers are gentleness and quietness. Will you stand by her; fortifying her strength even in the depths of Darkness?" Their query came unexpectedly and he twisted around to look back at them uncertainly.

All his life he had only ever considered himself. He was never responsible for another, nor did he ever concern himself with attending to another. Nevertheless, their question ignited within him something he had felt previously in quiet moments with her, but had not been able to name or fully comprehend. Turning around once more to gaze at her, he answered without facing them, directing his reply as much to her as to those who asked the question. "Yes, I will."

"As a Guardian, she has lived among the Temple inhabitants, sheltered and protected. She knows nothing of combat or brutality. Will you uphold her, even in the face of fear, evil, danger?"

He had not considered these things before asking her to help him, but he found no shred of doubt within him by answering once again that he would.

"Her ability to reach out to others is extraordinary, but leaves her fragile, uncertain, and very often overwhelmed. Will you share your strength of purpose, your tenacity and resilience with her where there are only shadows of confusion? Will you comfort her even when there is no comfort to be found?"

He paused, staring at her with an intense expression that required no words. After a moment, he nodded. "Yes, I will."

They stared at each other, transfixed, and nothing Veryth or The Elders might have said in that moment would have been heard by either. He said nothing to her, but the depth of emotion that suddenly overtook him told her more than any words he might have chosen. She too stood mutely, her heart hammering; yet no words could express the sensations spiraling inside her. Birdsong alone proclaimed the moment.

Lowering their heads as if by one consent, The Elders fell into silence and it was Veryth who spoke. He explained that many plans had yet to be considered, many details decided upon and many arrangements needed to be made before he could begin the perilous undertaking he proposed. He need not discuss the particulars of his plans, as they were made known to The Elders during The Prevailation when they had joined their thoughts with his in seeking the truth of his desires. During the coming hours, and perhaps days, they would focus on his plan, carefully preparing for any unforeseen eventualities, plotting tactics, and considering the appropriate measures of protection required. They would call for him, for Ayla and for whomever else he intended to assist him when their mediations were ended.

* * *

The friends sat together in the temple garden room, a place filled with green plants that grew lush in spite of the advancing season of ice and snow. Sunshine streamed in to warm the room through three walls made of thick paned glass, rather than of brick and mortar. These panes allowed every measure of warmth that might be conveyed from the diminished winter sun to pour into and warm the lovely space. Sitting among the verdant plants at low tables that made it possible for them to recline upon a multitude of silken cushions, they partook of the noontime meal with Mardan. Their conversation drifted over many topics, but ultimately turned to The Rite of Prevailation when Mardan insisted on being given a full account of the extraordinary event he had missed and he was not disappointed.

Released from the unbearable anticipation and uncertainty of awaiting Ayla's reply and truly happy for the first time in as long as he could remember, Gairynzvl embarked upon recounting his tale with such enthusiasm that even Ayla, who has witnessed the entire ceremony, listened as one mesmerized. Proving to be a surprisingly skilled storyteller, he captivated their full attention for the better portion of an hour, sharing openly the trepidations he had suffered prior to the ritual. He explained the startling effect the Light had had upon him and described the shocking sensations and pain he experienced with the final transformation in detail that left them staring back at him in dumb-struck silence.

During his account, Gairynzvl noticed Ayla's attention drift away on more than one occasion. Since she had been with him during the entire event, he was at first unperturbed by her lack of interest, but when she repeatedly fixed her gaze upon the empty air above or behind her and when she turned her head slightly to one side or the other with an expression of intense concentration as if she was fixedly listening for something he felt convinced he knew the cause of her distraction.

Ilys.

When he completed his tale and those around him sat quietly in stunned contemplation, he gazed curiously at Mardan and asked if he was weary or if he felt the need to return to the Nursing Ward to rest. At once, Ayla's attention returned to the moment and she, as well as Nayina and Reydan's vigilant gazes focused on their recovering friend. Sighing at their mutual fretfulness, Mardan shook his head and insisted that he was as comfortable there among the cushions as he would be in his bed and if they promised to take no offense should he drift off to sleep unintentionally, then he would much rather remain there with all of them. Nodding without a hint of surprise at the Celebrant's stubbornness, Gairynzvl drew a deep breath and turned his gaze to Ayla.

"Since you choose to remain, there is one further thing I must tell." Ayla's startled stare locked with his and he could easily hear the flutter of her indecisive thoughts, but he shook his head subtly at her. Nayina alone observed the manner in which they gazed at each other and the nearly imperceptible shake of his head and, at the sight, an idea began forming in her mind that she had not considered previously, though she said nothing. When he continued and spoke to Ayla as if answering something she had not spoken, she could not conceal the stare of fascination with which she then regarded them, realizing for the first time that they were able to communicate without the need for words.

"He must be told, Ayla, as must all your friends."

Shaking her head, Ayla vigorously disagreed, but even as they seemed to non-verbally argue the point, Mardan straightened and stared at them anxiously. "What must you tell? What must we be told?" The tremor in his voice betrayed all too clearly the fear this statement produced in him and Ayla could not help sensing the sudden rush of worry that arose within him. Before she could offer any further explanation, however, Gairynzvl turned his gaze to Mardan's and cerulean locking with icy lavender.

"I wish to return to The Uunglarda."

Chapter Nine

The utter astonishment that met his words was exemplified by Mardan's immediate reaction. Jumping up from his reclining position, any weariness that might have lingered within him vanished as he stepped instinctively nearer to Ayla. His impulse to protect her was still as strong as it had ever been and the sharp incredulity of his tone returned to what it had been the first time he and Gairynzvl had ever spoken.

"Have you lost your mind? Why, by all the Ancients, would you want to return somewhere from which you have spent nearly your entire life trying to escape?"

Shaking his head, Gairynzvl got to his feet as well, attempting to explain himself. "I do not wish to remain there."

Mardan stepped over the few cushions that lay scattered between them and spread his wings more assertively. "Why return at all, then? Has everything we have been through and everything Ayla has lost, been for nothing?" His antagonism had a predictable reaction. Frowning with mounting vexation, Gairynzvl flexed his own wings, which were equally as powerful as Mardan's, and stepped closer to the Celebrant to glare back at him belligerently.

"Your suffering is nothing compared to the torment of the Integration."

Mardan's eyes narrowed, the muscles in his jaw visibly tightening and he would have rebuked him explicitly, but Ayla leapt up as well, imploring him to listen to what Gairynzvl was trying to say. Turning to look down at her, his pause offered enough time for Gairynzvl to continue hastily.

"The torment suffered by childfey in The Uunglarda is unimaginable. *That is why I must return; to help any I can; to rescue as many as I am able and,*" he paused, doubtful of the wisdom in revealing Ayla's willingness to aid him, but certain that he could not conceal the fact. At least, not for very long. Mardan's expression had shifted from aggression to uncertainty and he was listening rather than mounting a verbal attack. Gairynzvl knew him well enough to realize that this might be his only opportunity to justify his argument. "I know the secret ways in and out of The Uunglarda. I am still capable of opening and closing portals. I know where the Dlalth sequester the newest younglings and where they lock childfey away as punishment. I am their best hope for rescue." He paused once again and swallowed with visible effort before he continued. "As is Ayla, which is why she has agreed to help me."

Nayina and Reydan gasped in dismay. She had to hold her companion back in the fear that he might also leap up to confront Gairynzvl, but the fierceness of Mardan's scowl that met these words were enough to make him step back from the Celebrant and lower his wings in a clear indication of deference. Despite this gesture, however, Mardan's exasperation would not be pacified. Staring down at Ayla, he directed his next question to her, rather than at the newly prevailed Dark One standing before him lest he reach to throttle him before he could gain control over his astonished disbelief. "You have already agreed? Without even speaking to me on the matter?"

She closed her eyes against the disappointment and resentment in his tone, unable to bear the heartache that poured out from him or the outrage. "I wanted to speak with you about it, Mardan, but The Elders required an answer this morning. I had to decide on my own."

He did not hesitate in his reply. "And while you were deliberating, did you give any thought to the immense danger involved? Did either of you consider what *will* happen to her if she is captured by Demonfey?" Shaking his head, Mardan glared at Gairynzvl with renewed hostility before turning away, but he followed the Celebrant closely and tried to make him understand.

"Yes there is danger. I cannot deny the truth of what you say and *should either* of us be captured we will surely pray for death long before it comes, but if you knew even a fraction of what happens to these childfey during the Integration you would understand why we feel compelled to try."

Mardan stopped and returned the Dark One's stare haughtily. "I know well enough what the Ancient Texts tell us," he began, but Gairynzvl scowled fiercely and moved even closer with a determined stride. Rebuking the fair Fey's complacent attitude with a tone of indignation that grew in intensity with each step he took, he nearly growled in reply.

"Really? What *do* these Ancient Texts tell you? Do they speak of the neglect these younglings endure? Do they describe the brutal physical abuse they suffer? Do they illustrate the vile acts of depravity that are visited upon even the most innocent?"

Those around him fell into dismayed silence, the imagery of his words spawning nightmarish contemplations in each of them, but he continued undeterred. "Do they tell of gnawing hunger and unquenchable thirst when you have not seen food or water in days? Do they describe the barbaric choices you are forced to make? Do they express the heartache or the anguish of knowing that all you once had is lost and those whom you thought loved you will *never* come to help you?" His voice shook with emotion. It did not shake with rage, but the piercing despair that betrayed unmistakably that he had suffered each of the unimaginable cruelties he described. In Mardan's horrified silence, he pressed his point further, like a blade that is forced deeper into an open wound. "I know how and where to find them. I remember the twisting ways that are designed to confuse. I can open portals and lead them out of the darkness and, although I can hear them and feel their anguish, only Ayla has the ability to See them as they truly are. Only she will be able to determine if they can be saved or if they are truly dangerous."

"Dangerous?" Nayina interjected with perplexed skepticism. "How can a childfey be dangerous?" Having listened in silence to their arguing, she found what he said to be incomprehensible and could not keep silent. Gairynzvl turned his lavender-ice gaze to her before answering, but his explanation clarified for all.

"Most little ones are capable of clinging to the Light much longer than you might imagine. Hope is a powerful motivator, even in the face of unthinkable cruelty; yet some cannot withstand the torment and the torture. Some seem to turn from the Light with frightening ease, twisting into monsters that even I would not cross. Those, sadly, are truly lost and best left where they are."

No one spoke as they contemplated what he told them, each appalled by the truth that had never been shared with them. Each one of them was moved to the depths of their being when considering such inconceivable brutality directed at toddlefey. In that stillness, the glimmering afternoon sunlight shifted and flickered for the briefest moment across a shadow that drew Gairynzvl's attention and compelled him to continue. "I can find them. I can open the way. Ayla can ensure our safety and can comfort the little ones in ways I cannot, but.... there is one other who can also help us. A Light Bender who can shield us from detection; who can hide us in plain sight."

"A Light Bender?" Ayla repeated, as astounded by this further pronouncement as the rest were, but Mardan interrupted acerbically before she could query any further.

"Benders of Light exist in legend only. Perhaps The Prevailation was more taxing upon you than you realize."

Tired of the Celebrant's ridicule, Gairynzvl scowled with an impulsive rush of anger and flexed his wings fiercely in an obvious display of animosity. Mardan reciprocated with an equal measure of hostility and Reydan shoved Nayina's hands aside and got up to stand beside him, his aura glowing crimson with constrained ire. Ayla and Nayina backed against the far wall, anticipating that at any moment the malefey would clash in a fearsome display of strength.

Without warning, a high-pitched echo of laughter resounded through the room, the sound causing all to look about with bewilderment; all, with the exception of Gairynzvl. Turning his head to the side, he could not help rolling his eyes or keep himself from sighing loudly with exasperation, but the moment he did, Mardan stalked forward and grasped him firmly by both shoulders. "You dare bring a Demonfey into the sacred Temple!"

Knocking his hands away forcefully, Gairynzvl spat back with marked sarcasm. "For a Fey who is dedicated as a Celebrant, your predilection for hostility is really quite unbelievable." It was an insult intended to infuriate and it had the desired effect. Beyond the restrictions of self-control, Mardan lashed out suddenly, striking his rival across the jaw with his clenched fist. The force of this attack instantly split Gairynzvl's lips, leaving blood upon the Celebrant's hand and he stared down at it with an unreadable expression as the shefey shrieked in dismay. Staggering backwards with both malefey in pursuit of him, Gairynzvl had to discover other means of defending himself without the weaponry of twelve inch spines upon his wings that he had grown used to.

Reydan swung powerfully, the force of his fist catching the reeling Dark One across the other side of his face, impelling him into a backward fall even as Mardan stepped forward to strike again. When he did, Gairynzvl unfurled his wings to their fullest and with one powerfully circular, backwards wing beat he managed to keep himself from falling. This action, however, left him standing, dazed and unsteady, before the incensed Celebrant who used his adversary's spinning equilibrium to his own advantage. Drawing back with determination, he delivered a punishing blow just below the ribs, causing Gairynzvl to double over with a breathless groan.

Rushing forward then, the two malefey kicked and swung at him ruthlessly, but the target of their hostility managed to beat his expansive wings another time and it was all he required. Using the momentum this motion supplied, Gairynzvl lunged forward, driving his head and shoulders into Mardan's stomach where bandages still wrapped his healing injuries. Lifting him upwards while hurling him backwards into Reydan, he was unprepared when Mardan screamed in pain. Dropping him and stepping back with an abruptness of motion that left Mardan sprawling, he watched with a brooding combination of satisfaction and guilt as the Celebrant tumbled to the floor and curled into a protective ball, wrapping his arms and wings around himself in distress.

Reydan hissed in rage and leapt at his distracted opponent, colliding into him and tumbling with him in a chaos of wings and limbs over the nearest table. As one Fey sought retribution, the other attempted to defend himself from the viciousness of the attack. During this calamity, the light within the room noticeably dimmed. Warping as if folding in on itself, it shattered outward in a burst of blazing radiance that streamed through the many panes of glass out into the graying afternoon and beamed into the Healing Ward just on the other side of the hallway. Stunned into momentary silence, all but one Fey blinked upward into the shimmering glow to behold a silver horned, dragon-winged shefey hovering above them. She shook her head in apparent disgust at their behavior and chided them brazenly.

"And you call us savage?"

The one who did not look upward lay back upon the hard wooden floor with his wings splayed wide. Covering his eyes with one hand and drawing a deep breath as he regained his senses, he sighed prodigiously and did not uncover his face before announcing with an unmistakably exasperated tone, "This is Ilys and, as you can see, she is a Light Bender."

Chapter Ten

Drawn by the sounds of shouting and conflict as well as the unexplainable radiance that poured into the Healing Ward, several attendant Healers rushed into the garden room to find the most shocking and unexpected scene. Tearful and uncertain Ayla and Nayina were kneeling beside Mardan who lay curled upon the floor groaning, his arms crossed over his abdomen and his wings tightly curled round himself in a clear sign of distress. Reydan stood at his other side, gazing down on him while absently nursing several bleeding cuts upon his face, neck and hands. Gairynzvl stood at the young Celebrant's feet, but was turned about and was watching the Healers who were hurrying into the room. The most startling sight of all, however, was the pallid, horned she-demon he held firmly by the arm.

When he saw her, one of the Healers stopped abruptly and turned back toward the corridor, his voice echoing down the passageway as he called for the closest Fey Guard. The two other Healers hastened to their work, one ministering to Mardan's renewed injuries while the other turned back to the Healing Ward where he called for a stretcher to return Mardan to his bed.

"What in the name of all that is sacred happened here?" Throwing back his hood in an extraordinary display of disapproval, the golden-haired Healer kneeling beside Mardan looked up at Reydan accusingly, but he only turned to gaze at Gairynzvl. He had raised his hand to wipe blood from his mouth and chin and met the Healer's intense viridian glare, but said nothing.

The Healer continued more accusingly, "he has but awoken from the depths of unconsciousness. Why have you attacked him?" His tone was not the characteristic soothing calm of a Healer, but held the unmistakable knife-edge of annoyance. Both malefey stared back at him, hesitant to respond, but it was not

Gairynzvl who finally answered him. In a breathless voice that all too clearly betrayed his pain, Mardan answered.

"He had just cause, Evondair." Looking beyond the Healer, Mardan's gaze captured Gairynzvl's who stood watching the injured Celebrant with a culpable expression and tightly folded wings. "Dark One, once again I have been too quick to judge you and have mistreated you abominably," he paused, groaning with the effort that speaking required, but before Gairynzvl could answer he drew a deep breath and continued. "It is I who had no just cause to attack. Can you forgive me?"

This apology and admission of guilt plainly startled him and Gairynzvl could not keep from shaking his head. "No." He answered, his deep voice filled with bewilderment.

Appalled that he would refuse such a sincere expression of regret, Ayla whispered his name sharply and, although the others did not speak, their mutual astonishment could not be concealed. Continuing to shake his head, Gairynzvl looked at Reydan and then back to Mardan. "No. We all reacted poorly, but, if we now better understand each other then there is nothing to forgive. Is there?" His question was so wholly uncertain while so entirely honest that neither Reydan nor the Healer who watched him with an intense stare could articulate a response.

Mardan returned his uncertain gaze with a dim smile. "Perhaps not."

At that moment, two tall Fey Guards entered the room, their golden armor glittering so strikingly that Ilys twisted in Gairynzvl's confining grasp, instinctively recoiling from them in fear. The Healer who stood waiting at the doorway pointed into the room without speaking, but the Guards had seen the Dark Fey instantly upon entering and were already hastening to seize her. Behind them, another pair of Healers entered, bearing the litter meant to return Mardan to his bed.

"'Rynzvl, don't let them take me," Ilys pleaded, her voice trembling with fear. Shaking his head at her, he retained his grasp on her arm and stepped in front of her, placing himself between the Fey Guards and their intended quarry. Speaking to the taller of the two Guards as assertively as he could manage without projecting hostility, he made an extraordinary request.

"She poses no threat, I assure you. Can you not leave her in my charge until I am able to explain her presence here to The Elders?"

Standing In Shadows

At his mention of the Three, the taller Fey stopped to consider his appeal even as the other continued forward, reaching to take her from his protective grasp. Ilys shrank back from him in horror, hissing at the Guard in an audacious display of ferocity even as Gairynzvl unfurled his broad wings to create a greater barrier between her and those seeking to apprehend her. "I will not allow you to take her." His deep voice bristled with opposition, causing the taller Fey to reach for his sword.

It was an action that brought shrill cries from both shefey who had taken refuge near the far wall once again, but which also gained the immediate attention of the Healer attending to Mardan. Rising from his kneeling position, Evondair turned to address the Guard in a diplomatic, but inescapably firm tone. "Regardless of the reason, you not permitted to draw you sword within the halls of The Temple."

This nuisance reminder clearly irritated the taller Guard, but he released his sword with little more than a curl of his lip as he stifled a hiss and stared back at Gairynzvl intractably. "I little understand how she managed to gain entry into the Temple, but I shall not leave this room without her."

Moving to stand within inches of him with an equivalent level of antagonism, Gairynzvl refused to back down and returned the Fey Guard's fierce stare without blinking. "Then you may not be leaving this room," he growled. Regardless of his newly Prevailed physical appearance, his instinctual reaction to any threat was confrontation and his indomitable bearing was undeniably daunting. With blood running fresh from the wounds to his lips and a laceration over one brow, the growl of his deep voice and the vicious glint of his icy stare were irrefutably unnerving. The two malefey stared at each other resolutely, neither willing to concede to the other.

"Bryth," Mardan said steadily, repeating the tall one's name more authoritatively after he was initially ignored. "Bryth!"

The Guard looked down at him doubtfully, then, realizing who was addressing him and taking note of his unexpected condition, answered with bewilderment. "What has happened here?"

Mardan shook his head, speaking breathlessly even as his pain visibly increased. "Nothing that has not already been resolved. Your vigilance to protect honors you, but do you not remember Gairynzvl?"

Bryth's gaze returned to the formidable Fey standing before him as he attempted to ascertain where they had met before, but he shook his head.

"You took us both from Ayla's cottage not more than a week ago," Mardan clarified and Bryth stared at Gairynzvl with renewed interest, shaking his head in disbelief.

"You are the Dark One I read?"

Barely able to recall the incident, Gairynzvl could offer no answer, but Ayla nodded and stepped closer, assuring them both that they had met on that terrible night and that Bryth had read Gairynzvl to ascertain his essence before he carried him from the light of the mirror. He had even tended to his injuries prior to the arrival of Healers. Neither fully accepted this as fact, but the Guard stepped back from him and prevented his companion from interceding any further. "There was a tale to be told on this matter and I should like to hear it when the time was more appropriate."

Satisfied that she was, for the moment, safe; Gairynzvl turned to Ilys with a raised a brow and released her from his grasp. He warned her to remain with them and not take wing or escape by shifting the light and she nodded briskly. Stepping away from him to a more dimly lighted corner of the room, she did not draw shadow to conceal herself, nor did she turn light over her head and vanish. As she withdrew, however, another quarrel involving Mardan ensued and she could not help staring in disbelief or muttering under her breath, "How can such an irksome Fey be a Celebrant?"

He and three of the Healers were arguing over his need to be carried back to his bed. Although he lay curled upon the floor in unmistakable pain, he insisted he was entirely capable of walking across the hall to the Healing Ward. They disagreed, pointing out that he could barely force himself to rise and that it was their duty to not allow him to undertake any action that might cause him further harm, but he shook his head emphatically and refused to roll onto the litter they had placed beside him. After listening for several moments with growing vexation, Gairynzvl stalked closer to the fray and waited for an opportunity to interject some sense into the dispute; yet, when no opportunity presented itself, he spread his wings wide and shouted to be heard over the vehemence of their disagreement.

"By the Ancients, Celebrant! You are as stubborn as a tryngalith in rut!" His outburst shocked them all into silence and Mardan could not mask the glare he shot at him, but in the stillness that met this exclamation Reydan could not contain his laughter. Mardan turned his glower upon his friend, prepared to rebuke him harshly as well, but even as he did Reydan stepped closer and hoarsely agreed with the Fey he had, only moments before, ferociously attacked.

"He does have a point."

"Brynnoch!" Mardan cursed in borrowed Dlalth, the word causing Gairynzvl to stare at him with astonishment that he should be familiar with so vulgar a word. Silence stretched tau between them, but even in his anger Mardan could not keep from laughing at the truth of their observations. As the others joined their tense mirth, he groaned as a shock of pain shot through him that drew his breath away.

Gazing down at him more good-naturedly, Gairynzvl stepped closer. "Now for mercy-sake, allow us to help you."

Gairynzvl only permitted the Healers to see to his own injuries after Mardan had been safely returned to his bed and the Healers had tended his wounds and Reydan's abrasions as well. The Healer who tended him was the same who had knelt beside Mardan and glared at him with palpable disapproval, but Evondair's demeanor had warmed slightly. He ministered to the Fierce One's needs while inquiring about the she-demon he had so unflinchingly defended, his tone once again calm and unobtrusive. "You know the she-Demon well?"

Gairynzvl nodded, but did not otherwise reply and Evondair looked at him more fixedly as he questioned further. "Have you known her long?"

Again, Gairynzvl only nodded, then locked his lavender-ice stare on the youthful Healer. "Does it matter to you?" His belligerence was barely constrained, but Evondair did not respond with matched hostility. Instead, he only nodded placidly as he applied a light balm to the cut on Gairynzvl's forehead.

"I only ask in the interest of safety. We are responsible not only for your lives, but many others who we tend within these walls." Gairynzvl glanced round them at the Healing Ward that housed only the three of them and shrugged.

"Others?"

Evondair's smile brightened. "There are other wards besides this one."

"She is no threat to you or anyone else." Gairynzvl's succinct reply made the Healer nod quietly, but he did not question further. When he had finished, he excused himself quietly and much of the remainder of the afternoon was spent in quiet converse beside Mardan's bed. Gairynzvl collected Ilys from a dim corner where she had retreated and brought her out into the diffuse light of the Healing Ward to meet those whom he now considered his friends. They greeted her hesitantly, openly uncertain about the horned she-Demon in their midst, but as the afternoon wore on, their conversation relaxed. When Mardan slipped into a late afternoon doze, the friends quietly dispersed leaving Ayla to tend him with Gairynzvl by her side and it was only then that Ilys, left unwatched at last, stole back into the shadows.

As the sun dipped towards the horizon, leaden clouds gathered in the diminishing light and spread thickly from the distant coastline, congesting together as if to consume the darkening sky. Although safe within the confines of the Temple, many of those within undertook preparations for what threatened to be the first storm of winter. They gathered livestock into protected grazing yards, shuttered windows and bolted them closed with braces, collected stores of wood indoors near hearths and cooking stoves, and collected extra candles to illumine the dark hours. Amid the flurry of activity as twilight descended the chanting of evening vespers drifted through the echoing corridors of the vast complex and Ilys could not keep from stalking irritably next to the closest door, longing to flee from the unfamiliar, placid environment.

Sensing her uneasiness, Ayla drew hesitantly nearer to her and offered the dubious consolation of new friendship against the isolation she felt pooling around her like dark waters. Gairynzvl watched them vigilantly, uncertain how the shefey might react to each other, particularly when Ayla discovered the truth about their past relationship, which Ilys would never be able to hide from her. His gaze never left them. Although he could hear every word they spoke, his trepidation was not alleviated when they neither argued nor taunted each other. They spoke together about the impending storm and the heartening comfort of being within the Temple and never touched on either of their relationships with him, but their quiet converse visibly unraveled him.

Watching his agitated pacing from beside the nearby hearth, Reydan strolled nonchalantly closer. "It is never a simple matter when the former greets the present." His observation was a riddle Gairynzvl comprehended perfectly, but, unable to influence or predict the outcome of the shefey's discussion, he sighed sharply and turned away. Moving past the dark haired, dark winged Fey, he gazed down at Mardan who lay quietly dozing.

"It is not simple at all," he muttered under his breath and, while he nodded concurringly, Reydan said nothing more on the matter. Outside, the wind moaned in the winter chill as if crying to be allowed inside where the warmth of plentiful fires lent the vast halls and corridors of the Temple an inviting and ruddy glow. The sound awakened unbidden memories in the depths of Gairynzvl's mind and, upon hearing it, he closed his eyes with a visible shiver.

"The winter wind bites shrewdly even through these protective walls," Reydan commented softly, fully cognizant that his new friend was not the least bit cold in spite of being neither telepathic nor empathic. In an attempt to shift the subject away from what he imagined had taken hold of his thoughts, Reydan continued more conversationally, "I am told, however, that the gales in the northern lands make our winters here seem temperate by comparison."

Turning his head, Gairynzvl gazed at him broodingly for a protracted moment, the intensity of his icy stare betraying the shifting tides of pain and anger within him. Shaking his head slowly then, as if trying to regain the focus of his thoughts, he turned back to face Reydan with an openly curious expression.

"The northern lands?"

The Fey of dark aspect nodded, smiling at his success as he moved closer to the fireside, casually inviting Gairynzvl along with him through a nearly imperceptible bend of one wingtip in the direction of the hearth. "Yes. It is brutal territory, I am told."

Gairynzvl's interest mounted and he queried further, drawing hesitantly closer to the blaze set beneath the Healing Ward's massive hearth, although he was still more than a little uncertain if such a conflagration would do him harm. "Who told you?"

"Rehstaed. I think you met him last night at the celebration. He is always about when Temple wine is on hand."

Grinning more easily at the mention of the agreeable Fey he had met and the thought of Temple wine, Gairynzvl inquired further, curious to know more about him and Reydan willingly shared his story, as far as he knew it.

Native to the north realm of Vrynnyth Gahl, he was once a captain of the Fey Guard stationed on the northern-most isle. Fierce of virtue and courageous of valor, he had thwarted more than a few attempted crossings by the Reviled, which were a common occurrence in those lands where many ancient pools of quiet water created glassy portals that were easily traversed. Unified with a beautiful shefey who had born him a son, the small family lived in the outlying countryside renowned for its loveliness, though it was quite far from any native settlements.

Reydan then explained that Fey Guard captains were often rotated through their various stations for the sole purpose of protection. If they were not frequently relocated, the Reviled would quickly discover where they made their homes and come seeking retribution for the wrongs they felt done to them, yet in such a far distant region rotation of The Guard was difficult to achieve. There simply were not enough Fey stationed there to make the practice feasible and, as a result, a legion of Dark Ones crossed over and located Rehstaed's cottage.

Even before he described what then occurred, Gairynzvl winced with bitter insight, but he did not interpose his own memories of similar events in which he had been forced to participate as a young Legionnaire. Reydan continued in a lower tone. His voice took on a heaviness of controlled emotion as he explained that the legion, numbering some twenty or more, bound him to a tree with leather lacings studded with spikes of metal designed to impede escape.

They then dragged his beloved from their home and brought her before him. Helpless to protect her, he was compelled to watch as they stripped and beat her and spent much time forcing such brutal acts of debauchery upon her that the life force within her was ultimately extinguished. His infant son had been bound in a sack to be taken with the Dark Ones into their realm, but in his monumental rage and anguish at having to witness the horrors visited upon his loved ones, Rehstaed dragged his hands through the jagged spines of his bonds, in spite of the injuries they inflicted, and attacked.

The sun was already rising. The Reviled could not linger, so, in order to distract him and ensure their escape, they tossed the sack that contained his only son down the cottage well. Although he tried countless times, he could not withdraw the body of his son from the depths of the well any more than he could restore breath to the body of his dreadfully abused beloved. Since that time, Rehstaed lived in Hwyndarin, but spent much of his time separated from them by his unbearable grief. Though many had tried to help him, including several Temple Healers, the only way he managed to tolerate continued existence was through the consumption of copious amounts of Temple wine. Comprehending his need, the Elders had ensured that a delivery of Temple wine was sent to his small cottage routinely.

Gairynzvl listened without interrupting, the icy glimmer in his eyes clouding with unanticipated emotion. He knew the merciless brutality of the Reviled only too well. He understood the helplessness of victimization and he thoroughly comprehended how difficult it was to scale the slippery slopes of the pit of despair. Nonetheless, through the sage counsel of Healers such as Veryth, he was also beginning to realize that through action, intercessory action that could aid another, he might find some measure of healing.

Gazing back at Reydan pensively, he posed one final question. "How far from this place is Veryn Falls?"

Chapter Eleven

Through the evening hours while the new friends shared a tentative meal together the descending storm outside continued to bolster its strength, shifting in the diminishing light from banks of gray clouds and wailing winds to thick mists of freezing rain that shrouded the forest in glazings of ice. As the night deepened and the temperature continued to plummet, the drapes of swirling, frozen mist became showers of sleet, driven into the depths of the forest and against the stone bastions and walls of the Temple by squalls of wind that rattled the braced shutters.

In the deep darkness of the storm, where the Reviled could cross unhindered by Light, many supplementary torches were lit, fires beneath hearths were set blazing, and candles, lanterns and glowing magic arts of every kind were kindled. When the others retired, settling down for the night in several of the unused beds of the Healing Ward because they had lingered too late to set off for home, Ilys huddled close to the fire fretfully. Nervous, even in the protected halls of the Temple, she felt certain her legion would come seeking her regardless of her location. Deep rooted fear gave her no alternatives except to forego sleep and remain vigilant, even when she saw how calmly Gairynzvl lay down in his own bed unhindered by concerns over dark shadows or slinking shapes in the ebon night. Yet even in her fear, when surrounded by the soothing quietness of the Healing Ward and the radiant warmth of its fire that crackled and sputtered blissfully within its massive hearth, she found she was unable to resist sleep.

During the mid-hours of night when the Temple halls stood silent and all those within slept peacefully except those Guards and Healers who were on duty, Evondair drew closer to the hearth where Ilys lay curled upon the floor like a cat sleeping in the ruddy glow of the fire. Without speaking, he drew the hood of his robe back and gazed down at her for many moments, the sheen of her silvery horns and dark dragon-hide wings awash in the flickering light. Long he stood regarding her as the storm howled and moaned outside, his golden hair glistening in the radiant firelight and the gleam in his deep viridian eyes indistinguishable. He sensed something about her that made him uneasy. Something he could not name, but did not trust in spite of the Fierce One's reassurances that she was no threat to them. At last, however, he withdrew as silently as he had approached.

The storm outside continued to gain ferocity during the deepest hours of the night as the winds doubled in intensity and gales of wintry coldness wreaked havoc amidst the frozen forest. Heavy in their gowns of glistening ice, many trees groaned and squealed in the onslaught of blustering wind, creaking and cracking in dismay. Heavy, blinding snow replaced the sprinkling sleet, accumulating rapidly in the bitter blow to tax the strength of their great arms and limbs and many bowed low in the tempest, overburdened.

Near the hour of dawn, a resounding rumble of thunder shook the Temple, jostling even the deepest of sleepers from their dreams. In the seconds of dazed confusion that followed, one of the mighty, ancient trees just outside the Temple garden room cracked and groaned vociferously. Swaying unsteadily, it came crashing downward in a chaos of shattering ice, splintering frozen branches and exploding panes of glass as it toppled in a deafening rumble through the garden room walls.

Awakened by this tumult and compelled into action by the frigid cold leaking into the Temple through the cavernous hole this wreckage created in the garden room wall, the friends assisted Fey Guards, Healers and Attendants alike in relocating many of the verdant plants and young trees that adorned the room to other areas of the Temple. Only when this was achieved and the room's furnishing removed to other areas were its heavy oaken doors closed against the bitter wind and blowing snow filling its spacious environment now laid open to the storm. Although the hour was still early, the fires of the kitchen were kindled to provide meals for those who had been obliged to rise early from their beds. As they waited, they returned to the massive hearth of the Healing Ward and gathered round it quietly in an attempt to fend off the chill that had robbed them all of the comforting warmth they had enjoyed during the night.

The day drug onward, the storm blustering and moaning in the leaden gray light as the winter tempest continued to gain momentum. It battered the forest with gale force winds while hurling ever deepening snow from the skies and the temperature hovered only a few degrees above freezing. Trapped indoors, the friends lazed the morning away in gloomy silence. They shared a quiet noontide meal, but barely spoke as they gazed out at the daunting blizzard and in the afternoon they wandered aimlessly through the vast halls and corridors of the Temple. As the afternoon progressed towards evening and the storm showed no signs of abating, Gairynzvl began restively pacing.

Fully aware that The Elders would summon him only when their meditations over the details of his plan were complete, he found waiting on their contemplations interminable. Unaccustomed to quietness, he was unable to find anything inside the Temple with which to distract his thoughts or any suitable way to release his pent up energy and frustration. He could not combat the vexation this delay caused in him any more than he could keep from flexing his wings in a most agitated manner as he stalked up and down the broad hall. Sensing his irritation, Ayla tried whispering to him through her thoughts, but he only hissed irascibly and turned away.

Watching him from beside the fire with half closed eyes, Ilys smiled perceptively and got slowly to her feet. Moving in a casual, directionless amble, she made her way across the room while attempting to draw as little notice to herself as possible. Ordinarily, she would have turned light round herself so her movements would go unnoticed, but she had not forgotten Gairynzvl's warning to remain visible with them. Should she slip into concealment, the Fey Guard would certainly consider such actions suspect and would have cause to take her into custody. Therefore, instead of winking into the unseen, she meandered quietly around the room, pausing here, sitting down there, until she reached the windows where he stood with his arms crossed over his broad chest and stared out with a brooding expression at the menacing storm.

He felt her approach and sighed sharply when she stopped beside him, but he said nothing. Shaking her head slowly, she gazed out into the baleful storm, searching the shadows for movement. "The snow conceals far too well. They could be anywhere," she observed quietly. Again he only sighed harshly. "It *is* a shame there is nothing else we can do but wait."

Understanding her suggestive comment perfectly, he closed his eyes against the sudden rush of desire that washed over him with as much force as the bluster just beyond the walls. Subtly, he shook his head. "We are within the Temple, Ilys," he whispered heavily, his response neither a rebuke nor a denial.

She smiled mischievously. "That did not stop you the other night."

Turning his head, he glared down at her petulantly, her temptations doing nothing to ease the frustration building inside him. Although he knew it would not be difficult for them to find a dark corner in which to lose themselves, he recalled only too vividly the emptiness of their last encounter. He had no means of explaining why, either to himself or to her, but he no longer desired the inconsequential sex they used to enjoy. Turning away from her without another word, he crossed the room with a purposeful stride to the small divan upon which Ayla was quietly reading. She was attempting to distract herself from intentionally listening to their conversation and gazed up at him with a glimmer of trepidation betrayed in her amber eyes, but she was unprepared when he took away the scroll she held and pulled her to her feet. Without speaking, he continued toward the door and, although every gaze in the room followed them, the weight of their stares did not impede his actions. Astonished by his brazenness, yet undeniably curious, Ayla willingly followed him out into the hallway. When they were no longer the object of everyone's attention, however, he did not do what she anticipated he might.

"I am going to Veryn Falls to seek out Rehstaed." His announcement both startled and confused her. Stammering to catch up with his racing thoughts, her queries formed before she could speak them so that he responded before she could verbalize her misunderstanding. "I cannot abide all this waiting, all this quietly sitting and doing nothing. We need others to help us liberate the childfey. We cannot hope to succeed on our own. Reydan has told me how fierce Rehstaed was as a Fey Guard and I think he could make a formidable ally."

Gazing up into his eyes in the dim light of the corridor, she could not hide the concern his decision stirred in her. "That may be so, but to go now in the deepest hour of the storm. Is that wise? You do not know the way. How will you keep from becoming lost?"

Expressing his annoyance in the only manner presently available to him, he hissed petulantly and turned aside. "I must do *something*," he growled under his breath, as much to himself as to her. Although she could easily feel his irritation, understanding of his emotions did not alleviate her anxiety. Shaking her head, she tried again more forcefully.

"Going out alone into a winter tempest is not going to help you."

Rounding on her suddenly, he prepared to rebuke her, but as he drew back his wings in an assertive stance he heard a voice in his thoughts that caused him to pause and look round in surprise.

Do not be a fool!

Standing guard unseen at the next passageway, Bryth could hear their argument without effort and readied himself to defend Ayla should the newly prevailed Dark One act rashly. Though he did not speak, he could not quiet his thoughts that answered Gairynzvl's impulsive actions. Seeing him arch his wings aggressively, Bryth turned sharply from his post and approached the pair with a purposeful stride. "Go in the morning, Fierce One," his low voice caused Gairynzvl to face him and his antagonistic demeanor intensified.

"What did you call me?" he snarled at the tall Guard as he came to stand within inches of him.

"Fierce One," Bryth answered evenly, unprepared when Gairynzvl shook his head and glared back at him even more crossly.

"That is not what I heard."

Bryth's eyes narrowed as he regarded the malefey before him who stood nearly as tall as he. His physique was equally as powerful as his own and his confident bravado was unwavering. "Then you are perceptive, indeed," he answered with a subtle nod, clearly discerning the Fierce One's ability to read his thoughts without the need to further test the issue. They glared at each other for an intense moment and Ayla could not keep from backing away fearful that their terse conversation might come to blows, but a crooked grin turned the corner of Bryth's mouth and he visibly relaxed. "If you want something to do tonight, join me."

Perplexed, Gairynzvl did not answer.

"Several Guards who are off duty, as well as a few Healers who are no longer needed this eventide, will be playing Vladokhyssum."

Again, Gairynzvl did not respond, though his expression wavered from aggression to uncertain curiosity.

"Ever play?" Bryth inquired in the hope of drawing him in, but when Gairynzvl immediately glared at him with resentment he stepped back and raised his hands in a gesture of self-accusation. "Forgive me. Now who is the fool?" Revealing in this innocuous manner that he comprehended Gairynzvl's gift of telepathy he shook his head at his blunder and tried again. "One of my teammates was injured when last we played and cannot compete tonight. You would make a formidable replacement and I suspect you would enjoy the game. Immensely." He chose his words with cunning and was not disappointed with the reaction they produced.

"Vladokhyssum?" Gairynzvl repeated uncertainly and Bryth nodded, but it was Ayla who answered.

"It is also known as Crucia Fynnowyn."

Gairynzvl turned to look down at her with disbelief. "Kill the Fey?" The incredulity of his tone made the tall Guard laugh devilishly.

"No one has ever actually been killed. That would make continued play problematic as it would be a bit difficult finding willing replacements," he explained amid his own laughter and his mirth was infectious. Relaxing his guarded stance at last, Gairynzvl laughed as well and the charming sound caused Ayla to gaze up at him with open affection.

Bryth continued despite the fact that the Fierce One had not yet agreed to play. "The rules are simple; competition is challenging and escaping unscathed is difficult, but it beats doing nothing." Again, his description was artfully delivered and he could plainly see Gairynzvl's interest was piqued. "We play at the hour of seven. If you are interested, meet me at the court at six so I can explain the rules to you. If you decide to join us, we will have time to find you something to wear." Bryth paused and leaned nearer. "If not, you can return to the Healing Ward and sit by the fire with the shefey." His words were meant to taunt, but his smile never faltered and Gairynzvl only laughed louder at his jeering. Nodding with satisfaction, Bryth reminded Ayla where to find the court in which they would play before he turned away and moved back towards his post. Pausing after a few strides, however, he twisted round to add one final enticement.

"Bring Reydan as well. If you are injured and cannot continue, he can finish out the round in your stead."

Chapter Twelve

Within the hour all of the friends, including Mardan who insisted that he was well enough to observe, if not compete in, a game of Vladokhyssum, arrived at the vast indoor courtyard specifically designed for the game. The building was an immense circle many hundreds of feet in diameter and height, its broad ceiling supported by arches of intricate metalwork. The grass playing field was well tended and green, stretched the entire circumference of the arena, and had at its center a tall shaft some fifty feet high, which supported a ring seven feet in diameter. The walls of the arena housed equidistantly mounted torches that provided ample lighting and had three broad sliding doors at ground level, which could be opened or closed for cooling and ventilation.

Standing near the center of the field, Bryth awaited the arrival of the Fierce One. He was immensely pleased with himself for his discovery of what he considered a valuable new player and was anxious to include him in the game, certain he would be a fearsome competitor. When the entire group arrived, he greeted them heartily, particularly Mardan whom he had known throughout his many years of study to become a Celebrant. In spite of his geniality, however, he was quick to begin Gairynzvl's instruction and drew him away from the others as he described the game in better detail. Gairynzvl listened intently, eager to learn.

"There are four teams, each consisting of four players and one replacement. Play begins on the ground, but once the ball is in motion, no part of your body is allowed to touch the ground. The object is to score goals by getting the ball through the central goal ring by any means possible."

"*Any* means?" Gairynzvl clarified and Bryth nodded.

Standing In Shadows

"You can throw it, kick it, drop it, pass it to a closer teammate or, if you can manage it, you can fly through the ring carrying it, though I would not advise that particular maneuver until you have had a great deal of practice." Looking up at the goal ring, he illustrated how dangerous this might be by taking to wing in order to show him just how small the ring was in comparison to the length and breadth of his wings.

Alighting once again, he then continued. "Play continues unbroken until either someone scores or the ball hits the ground. Each player of one team must score once in order to gain victory, which sounds simple enough until you understand that while you are carrying the ball, twelve other players will be doing everything in their power to keep you from scoring and the only defense you have is your three teammates." With this explanation the true challenge of the game became clearer, as did the game's less than official name, kill the fey. Regardless of the hazards involved, or perhaps because of them, Gairynzvl could not hold back a brazen smile and Bryth nodded at his obvious appreciation of the games inherent peril.

"Sounds amazing." Gairynzvl note with evident eagerness and Bryth nodded with equal enthusiasm.

"There are, of course, a few simple rules designed for protection. You cannot *intentionally* knock your opponent over the head. You cannot kick him, bite him, or tear his feathers out." He paused, nodding while waiting for Gairynzvl's reaction to these straightforward rules, but his reaction was to wait as well, clearly supposing there were additional rules yet to come. When Bryth did not continue, Gairynzvl could not contain a skeptical chuckle.

"Is that all? Those are the rules?"

Bryth nodded with a smile of wry delight. "If you *intentionally* break one of these rules or if you touch the ground during play you are sent into exile." He turned with this pronouncement and pointed at a small, bare patch of ground at the far side of the arena. "Your penalty is to sit out two plays, which can sometimes mean two points, and *that* will make enemies of your teammates faster than scoring will make rivals of your opponents."

The ferocity of the game was becoming very clear; still, the appeal of the contest was irresistible and even before the tall Fey Guard could inquire if he was still interested in playing Gairynzvl looked down at his leather clothing doubtfully. "Surely I cannot play in this?"

Agreeing that he could not, Bryth revealed that he had already made provision for him by bringing one of his own spare uniforms in the hope that he would find the game enticing. Collecting Reydan along the way, he then showed them the team rooms where they could change and he could introduce them to their fellow players.

As these things took place, the outer circle of the arena began to fill with excited spectators and the remaining friends found places where they could sit along the field's perimeter to watch. Healers, Celebrants, Guards, Scholars, Artisans, as well as a few enthusiastic villagers who were not put off by the blizzard still howling outside all gathered to enjoy the event. Even Ilys, who had accompanied the friends somewhat begrudgingly, found the excitement and anticipation of the growing crowd contagious. Relaxing for the first time among The Fey of The Light, she spoke cheerfully with Ayla and Nayina, putting her own competitive nature to the side, if only for the moment. Yet when the contestants began to emerge onto the field, such a chaos of cheering and whistling ensued, include strident trills and trebles of wings, that she could not keep from cringing in surprise. Until, that is, she saw the players.

Each player wore a form fitting uniform made of comfortable material that hugged the body, but stretched and moved easily. Close fitting pants with a belt cinched round the waist and lacings in front accentuated the player's trim, athletic physique. A sleek, short-sleeved shirt made of similar material was worn tucked into the pants, and boots, which came up to the knee, matched the specific color of each team's uniform. There was red with a black blaze down the side of each leg; white with a golden blaze; and blue with a white bolt of lightning in place of a blaze. Then Bryth stepped out of the shadows of the team room tunnel, followed by his fellow teammates who all wore a black uniform that boasted an abstract red and white dragon snaking up each leg instead of the customary blaze. At their emergence, the boisterous noise of the crowd doubled.

Beside her, Ayla grew silent and Ilys could not keep from turning to watch her when Gairynzvl stepped out of the shadowy tunnel. Clearly appreciating the vision he presented in the tight, fitted uniform that hugged every toned and muscular inch of his body in the most complimentary fashion, she could not take her gaze from him nor keep herself from sighing out loud in spite of the fact that Mardan sat only a few feet away.

Standing In Shadows

There was no ceremonious preamble, just the raw excitement of the spectators and the evident enthusiasm of the players who gathered on the north side of the field. There they took several moments to stretch in preparation for the game as well as to flex their wings aggressively, posturing and swaggering audaciously in front of their rivals with visible defiance. Gairynzvl, however, prepared for the game more shrewdly. Attentively observing the others while he stretched his body and flexed his expansive wings repeatedly, he never gave a moment's indication of his underlying ferocity.

Only when all members of the teams agreed they were sufficiently prepared did they gather into a loose circle with the captain of one team standing in the center of that ring holding the ball. The ball, which was little more than corded rope covered in soft leather perhaps ten inches round, was then tossed high into the air and play began.

As the crowd erupted into raucous cheering yet again, all sixteen players launched themselves from the ground in the first contest to see who would end up with the ball. At first sight there seemed to be no strategy to their endeavor. Each player sought to take hold of the ball while blocking the others from attaining it or to protect the ball in their possession and attempt to maneuver towards the central goal ring. However, it soon became obvious that maintaining possession was as difficult a task as succeeding in getting the ball through the goal ring. Players hurled themselves into the carrier trying to knock it loose, or delivered smart slaps with their wings designed to daze and confuse, or brazenly took hold of the ball in order to wrench it from the hands of the carrier all while deftly maneuvering upon the wing.

Ayla watched entranced as Gairynzvl joined in the fray, having never witnessed him flying before and mesmerized by his ability. Powerful, not only in his physique, but also in the manner in which he moved through the air, it quickly became evident that he was as skilled as any of the players there regardless of the fact that he had never played the game before. Twisting and darting with dexterity, he was able to build incredible speed with only a few wing beats. He was also fearless in the face of players even larger of physique and wingspan than his own and it took him only a few moments to gain control of the ball.

When he did, Bryth and the other two members of Team Dragon drew round him protectively as he paused briefly to orient himself, located the goal ring and then rushed with astonishing speed at the spire. Hard pressed to keep up with him, his teammate's incapacity left him unprotected and gave three other players the opportunity to charge at him from both the right and left direction at once. Watching breathlessly, Ayla cringed and covered her face, peeking through her fingers in spite of her fear that the impending collision would be calamitous, but no one was prepared for his reaction to the onrushing threat.

During the last possible seconds as the three opponents raced towards him, he spread his wings wide and with several vigorous, backward wing beats nearly halted his forward momentum altogether. Failing to anticipate such a tactic, the three attackers pummeled into each other, rather than into him. Hovering over them with a taunting laugh at their chaotic mishap, he then vaulted past them and continued towards the goal with his teammates now close beside him. When he was within twenty feet of the ring, he righted himself briefly in the air, tossed the ball upward and struck it with the tip of one wing to send it hurtling through the goal unimpeded.

The watching crowd went wild with exuberance. Bryth and his fellow teammates shouted with gleeful amazement at his talent, clapping him over the shoulders, tousling his shimmering hair roughly, and laughing heartily as they descended to the ground. No respite was taken. Only one interval of rest was given for every four plays. Thus, the players gathered once again into a loose circle, this time at the south side of the field with a new captain of one of the teams in the center of the circle. Shouting defiantly, he tossed the ball high into the air again and play continued.

Now on the defensive, Gairynzvl's undaunted guardianship of his fellow teammates was relentless. After many attempts, Bryth was next to take control of the ball and he and Gairynzvl flew so rapidly towards the goal spire that only two others managed to keep up. Although they were as swift as he, Gairynzvl lost track of the second adversary when that defender flew upward unexpectedly. He then plummeted down at them with the speed of a Dvarian raptor, forcing Gairynzvl to swerve away from Bryth's side in a tumbling confusion that nearly sent him careening into the ground. Recovering before any part of his body made contact with the grassy turf, he was nonetheless effectively eliminated from that play. In spite of this, Bryth was able to toss the ball through the goal ring to add another point to their score before being pummeled by his opponent.

Alighting breathlessly, the players moved to the east side of the field and formed their circle yet another time around a third captain. Leaning their hands upon their knees, some players panted heavily in a hasty attempt to recover before play continued, but the captain of Team Thunder, the team in blue, took advantage of their weariness and hurled the ball into the air as quickly as he could manage, recommencing play before any could sufficiently catch their breath.

Several times during this round other players took control of the ball, but none were successful in reaching the goal ring before being jostled forcefully by an opponent so that possession of the ball repeatedly changed. Play persisted unbroken as the combatants tested each other's resilience and perseverance, yet after many long minutes of uninterrupted play several rivals faltered. Colliding into each other in a disarray of wings and limbs, their mishap sent one player tumbling downward into the ground. The force of his impact sent a shocked gasp through the watching crowd and when he did not move to get up the remaining players quietly alighted while attendant Healers hurried to his side.

Breathless, Gairynzvl watched from a doubled over stance with his hands resting on his thighs and his wings pitched downward in fatigue. Waiting for the unfortunate Fey to awaken with Bryth and his teammates beside him similarly panting, he watched the unmoving Fey with distracted anxiety. It was only a few moments, but the silence in the courtyard instilled in each one present the undeniable jeopardy of their recreation. No one spoke.

When he finally regained consciousness, the Fey was cheered off the field and his replacement came into the game. The players assembled into another circle on the west side of the field and the captain of the remaining team took the ball. Launching it upwards, he followed it with such a burst of unanticipated speed that his weary opponents did not have time to catch up. In only a moment, the captain of Team Glyndyn, or Golden in the common tongue, had possession of the ball and was darting towards the goal ring with blinding speed. This was his particular gift and most of the other players wearily accepted his score as compulsory since it was largely unavoidable, but the opportunity the lack of pursuing opponents offered was too good to ignore.

Team Dragon shot after him. Gairynzvl's speed did not quite match his own, but what he lacked in swiftness The Fierce One made up for in brashness. Charging at the captain of Team Glyndyn in a headlong, unswerving attack, he never slowed his progress or gave any indication that he would slow down. Rushing at him aggressively, the other Fey abandoned his course towards the goal ring and twisted both left and then right in an attempt to escape. Even as Gairynzvl's pursuit deterred him from his course to the goal, Bryth and his teammates rushed towards them, then past them to position themselves in a straight line to the spire.

Ascertaining their scheme, the captain of Team Thunder shouted to the others to take up the defensive and eleven determined Fey headed straight for them. Gairynzvl tracked the captain of Team Glyndyn relentlessly, matching his tumbling shoulder rolls, mirroring his dexterous alterations in flight when he began in one direction and then shot unexpectedly in another. With each change, the captain got further and further away from the goal while Gairynzvl, in single-minded pursuit, doubled his wing beats. Effectively increasing his speed until he was hurtling recklessly at the ball carrier, the captain of Team Glyndyn did the unthinkable.

Before the newcomer could crash into him in a collision that would have knocked them both unconscious, he threw the ball vehemently at his opponent and Gairynzvl had only seconds to react in order to keep from being struck full in the face. Extending his hands in front of him, he lowered his head and sought blindly to catch the ball even as he twisted into a spiral roll. The ball struck his hands, then slipped through them into the feathers of his wing, which he curled forward hastily to encircle the sphere and direct it back into his hands.

Tumbling through the roll haphazardly, he righted himself, located Bryth, tossed the ball to him, and then plowed headlong into the first defender he found to protect the forward progress of the ball. Bryth twisted in the air and, before being struck by a defender, but he managed to pass the ball to his teammate. He was driven violently backward by another defender, yet somehow he managed to pitch the ball forward to the fourth member of their team and he tossed it through the goal ring.

The breathless teams descended to the field while riotous excitement poured from the spectators, though none of the players paid the uproar any heed. Panting vigorously or doubling over in an attempt to catch their breath or collapsing onto the ground to lie gasping for air, the players regrouped. Only one point needed to be scored by Team Dragon in order to gain victory, but this fact produced even greater determination in the other teams. The rest interval was three minutes. Long enough to regain control over their breathing, yet certainly not long enough to feel in any way recovered before having to form their circle on the north side of the field once more.

Resolute, yet undeniably weary, the players fought for control of the ball and throughout the next several plays two other teams managed to score. With the excitement of the crowd intensifying and the fatigue of the players escalated. Collisions became more frequent and the ball was dropped to the ground repeatedly forcing the players back down to the field in order to begin again and two additional players sustained injuries that left them unable to continue. Fresh replacement players, however, meant wings that were not tired and eager boldness of action that required team members to join forces in order to prevent additional goals. After four grueling rounds of play, the second rest interval saw nearly all the players lying down on the field in exhaustion.

Lying on his back with his broad wings splayed out beneath him, Gairynzvl breathed heavily, his eyes closed as he fully enjoyed the delicious weariness of exertion and the challenges of the game. Beside him, Bryth also gasped heavily, but he turned his head towards the Fierce One next to him and, although he could not speak, suggested through thought alone how they might attain the final score they required. Turning his head to gaze back at him, Gairynzvl grinned and nodded impishly, then turned to speak quietly to the player lying at his other side while Bryth did the same.

Assembling yet another time in their circle, Bryth once again stood in the center of the ring holding the ball. Looking at each of his teammates pointedly, he nodded to each of them to make sure they were aware of their plan and received subtle nods in answer. At this, all four of them began growling ferociously and when Bryth tossed the ball upward they followed after it so rapidly that they immediately took possession. Chased closely by the others, they drew together in such a tight formation that wings struck other wings and feathers flew. Rushing straight for the goal, they then began passing the ball between them so that each member of the team only held the ball for a few seconds.

Effectively protecting possession of the ball by relinquishing it to each other again and again, they hurtled in a mass of united wing beats and scattering feathers towards the goal and, although several other players forced their way into their formation, tracking the advancement of the ball was nearly impossible. As they approached the goal, Gairynzvl took the ball and arced upward, racing towards the ceiling of the arena while his team members continued the ruse of passing the ball. This deception confused several of the remaining players so that they tumbled into each other or stopped to hover through great effort in an attempt to decipher who actually had possession. Only one player followed Gairynzvl; the captain of Team Glyndyn.

Charging after him with blinding speed, he was unprepared when Gairynzvl folded his wings and came plummeting down at him in a stoop that made the crowd shriek in horror. Not intimidated, the captain continued upward, reaching outward as they neared each other in an attempt to break the other's descent, but with a slight correction of wing Gairynzvl shot passed him and headed straight for the goal spire.

The crowd began to scream wildly. He could not score again, he had already scored once. What was he doing? In his nearly uncontrolled plunge from the heights, Gairynzvl bared his teeth at the opponents waiting for him, growling so loudly that several broke off at the last second in the fear of being struck by him and smashed into the ground. Several others banded together in an attempt to stop him at any cost, but even as they grouped together in front of him, he moved the ball from under his arm. Undaunted by the wall they formed, he leaned into a roll and careened by them, flying directly at the fourth member of their team who waited near the goal spire.

The captain of Team Glyndyn had anticipated this action and came streaking downward from above, hurtling himself full force into Gairynzvl even as he reached the final member of their team who still had to make a goal. In their violent collision, the ball escaped his hands and bounced precariously off one of their knees as they tumbled chaotically downward. Rushing headlong after them, his teammate twisted in the air and caught the descending ball. Spinning leftward to avoid colliding with a defender, he darted with all the strength he still possessed towards the goal and threw the sphere sideways into the ring even as he shot past it and was struck by another player.

Gairynzvl and the captain of Team Glyndyn somersaulted and twisted wildly, breaking their speed with powerful wing beats as much as they were able before tumbling onto the ground and rolling in opposite directions. Feathers fluttered downward around them. Their teammates descended amid shouts of elation and concern while the crowd watched in horrified silence, waiting to see if either of them would move.

The captain stirred first, raising his fist skyward to the delight of the crowd, but they did not break into unprecedented cheering until Gairynzvl also moved. Drawing in a deep breath, he opened his eyes woozily and gazed up at Bryth who stood over him, looking down at him worriedly. Smiling brazenly he said in a breathless tone,

"Beats doing nothing."

Chapter Thirteen

After so turbulent a game, it was customary for all the teams to enjoy a celebratory drink together in the local tavern in order to ensure camaraderie among them. In preparation, they returned to the team rooms and Bryth showed Gairynzvl one of the luxuries afforded them by the Temple artisans: an extravagance they all appreciated immensely. Winding through the far end of the team rooms like an undulating serpent, a rivulet of fresh water poured through a series of artificially constructed waterfalls, splashing cool water invitingly. Cleansing, refreshing, and exceptionally soothing to weary muscles and wings, the rivulet rushed through sixteen coves where tumbling water created an environment more opulent than anything Gairynzvl had ever experienced.

Bryth left his side hurriedly, keen to enjoy the splashing water for himself while Gairynzvl stood and stared at the lavish private cove in disbelief. Life in the Uunglarda was harsh in every respect and never in all the years he was trapped there could he recall such an abundance of clean water. There, clean water was a luxury that many were regularly denied and obtaining it was exceedingly costly. Unintentionally, his thoughts returned to the darkness of that place. He recalled the many times he had stood in the icy rain shivering violently as he funneled rainwater with his wings into a stolen clay jar so he might have drinking water when he needed it, regardless of the fact that by doing so he would be miserably cold for hours.

Forcing these thoughts from his mind with a shake of his head, he reached behind him to unlace the shirt he wore from around his wings and pulled it off. The cool spray of the tumbling rivulet breathed a delicious chill across his skin and he could not keep from sighing at its touch or hurrying to remove the rest of his uniform. Stepping uncertainly, then, beneath the delicious cascade of water, he was unprepared for the overwhelmingly enticing, sensual delight of the soothing torrent. Tilting his head upward, he allowed the cool water to splash over his face and sighed once again, even more deeply. For long moments he stood beneath the crystalline 'plashing water, intoxicated beyond measure by the revitalizing current pouring over his head and through his hair, streaming across his skin, and deluging his feathers. Turning slowly in the rushing downpour, he closed his eyes and held out his hands, allowing the abundantly flowing water to spin his senses.

Enraptured beneath the waterfall's blissful caress, he stood in its voluptuous embrace, lost in the mesmerizing haze of its cooling touch. Despite the pleasure of his reverie, however, he could not combat the memories he had just shaken off when they sprang unexpectedly from the murky place where they waited. Their sudden onslaught caused him to sway unsteadily, squeeze his eyes tightly closed and bare his teeth in an effort of resisting them. Raising his hands to lean upon the stones that formed the wall of the cove, he fought the acutely painful memories assaulting him, perplexed by their startling intensity and distressing clarity. In the tumbling, chaotic darkness of his thought for the briefest moment, he felt surrounded.

In spite of the horror that pressed in on him from all sides, an impatient outcry by his teammates broke through the tide of bitter emotion and panic unexpectedly besetting him. Railing against his loitering, their good-natured jests and jeering prompted him to forcefully clear his senses, although doing so was as difficult as clearing ones head after enjoying too much wine. Pushing back the persistent, harrowing thoughts engulfing him, he stepped from the pleasing rush of water and shook his wings vigorously to dry them. Returning to the present moment with all due haste in order to put an end to the incessant protests and good-natured taunting of his fellow teammates, he dried himself quickly and got dressed. Aided by a malefey attendant who laced his shirt, vest and coat around his broad wings, his final appearance in the team room common area brought only further taunting banter, but as all were impatient for honey-mead, his new friends did not remain thusly employed for long.

The tavern in which they soon found themselves was cozy, warm and filled near to bursting with the villagers who had watched the game. Eager to offer their congratulations to Team Dragon and to meet the newcomer who had played so fiercely, these locals chattered excitedly amidst the teams and recounted the amazing plays they had witnessed, repeatedly calling for cups to be refilled when the honey-mead grew scarce. Amusing, congenial and in no way vulgar or raucous, the jovial atmosphere and bounteous laughter was delightful, though oddly alien, to Gairynzvl who found himself standing quietly to one side watching the goings-on with a brooding expression more than a few times.

He, in turn, was watched by Ayla, who, along with Reydan, Nayina and Mardan had joined the teams in their celebration. Sitting at a table near one of the tavern windows, she could not hear his thoughts over the boisterous exuberance of the malefey, but even without hearing him she could sense something was wrong. Unwilling to draw attention to him in the midst of so many new friends, she sat quietly and watched him attentively while trying to make sense of the roiling sensations she perceived from him.

As the mead took its beguiling effect and the tumbling of his confused and melancholic thoughts subsided, he smiled and laughed more unreservedly. His relaxed manner drew the others to him, including both Mardan and Reydan who left the modest converse of the shefey in order to enjoy carousing with him and his teammates and the remaining hours of the night slipped away. Nevertheless, even amidst the mirth and high-spirited antics the malefey enjoyed, Ayla remained aware of an underlying tension that seemed to be growing within him. It was nagging and unrelenting, though he gave no outward indication of distress and joined the jeering banter and mirthful revelry of his new friends.

When at last they returned to the Healing Ward where their beds were still made ready for them, Ayla found sleep difficult to attain. Heedful of the fact that Mardan lay only a few feet from them, Gairynzvl did not speak to her before taking to his bed, although once there he did whisper softly to her through his thoughts, causing more than a few sighs to escape her smiling lips before he drifted into exhausted sleep and left her on her own.

The hours of the night then twisted into a nightmare as her mind filled with images from his dreams that she could not escape. Although he slept, his memories grew active, filling his otherwise unoccupied mind with appalling brutality and terrifying cruelty that tormented her and kept her from sleeping. Finding it nearly impossible to disconnect from the shocking clarity of his unconscious thoughts, she tossed and turned for what seemed like hours. When she was least aware of it, sleep stole forward and trapped her in the same nightmare that ensnared him.

Darkness curled like billowing smoke. Shadows writhed like serpents and icy, ashen rain fell in a heavy mist from the leaden, sulfurous sky. It was bitterly cold, and a gnawing sensation of hunger and thirst filled each moment. Misery hemmed in like an inescapable shroud and the desolation of loneliness that filled each breath was unbearable. Tossing her head, Ayla moaned out loud and, as if to reiterate that despondency, Gairynzvl hissed sharply though bared teeth. At the far corner of the Healing Ward, Evondair raised his head from the pages of a book he was reading. Such sounds were enough to make him place the book down and move quietly towards the sleeping Fey.

Caught in the swirling darkness, the heavy murk made even the simplest actions burdensome and as they moved through the gloom, each breath became difficult. A sensation of being smothered descended upon them and Ayla gasped repeatedly for air, both within the realm of the nightmare as well as the peaceful environs of the Healing Ward. Shaking his head in an attempt to escape the suffocating sensation, Gairynzvl groaned deeply and drew a heavy breath.

Moving closer, Evondair watched them curiously as he debated the judiciousness of waking the sleeping pair. His gift was neither telepathy nor empathy as were the gifts they shared and determining whether the dream they apparently shared was pleasant or disagreeable to them was not a simple matter. Unconvinced, he stood quietly waiting.

Abruptly the shadowy streets and stifling gloom disappeared and in its place an echoing, damp cavern yawned before them, cold and vast. Immediately they sensed they were not alone, regardless of the fact that the dimness surrounding them was nearly impenetrable. Compelled to move forward into the gloom, Gairynzvl stretched out his senses in a manner entirely unfamiliar to him, as if casting a net into dark waters. Ayla paused and reached out with her hands, feeling for those around her. Shadows shifted in the engulfing darkness and they both could sense the ones waiting there, timid, terrified and alone. He pointed into the blackness and Ayla could not contain a sob of bitter anguish.

The sound filled the peaceful tranquility of the Healing Ward and was more than enough to persuade the attentive Healer that it was, indeed, a nightmare they shared. The distressing sound also roused Mardan from sleep and he got up quickly to join Evondair beside her bed, but although they both gently shook her in an attempt to waken her the nightmare held her captive.

Gairynzvl cringed violently. The images assaulting his thoughts became so inescapably harrowing that he grasped his pillow tightly with both hands and growled. Mardan turned to watch him, bewildered until the realization that they were sharing the same nightmare became as undeniable as the knowledge that the former Dark Fey and his love had grown close in a manner he had never shared with her.

Stopping in the blinding darkness, Gairynzvl heard innumerable steps coming towards them in the echoing silence of the cavern. They were small steps, the sounds pattering around them in spite of the fact that they could see nothing. Then a scream of pain shattered the darkness accompanied by a blurred and twisting image in his mind of a childfey in the brutal clutches of a Legionnaires. Gairynzvl hissed in rage, desperately seeking to find the youngling in the blackness, but what he saw was not actually taking place. It was a memory, though not one of his own. Ayla shrieked at the sight as it filtered through to her as well. Grasping onto him so tightly that he stumbled and clung onto her in return, they stood unable to move in the dreadfully blank vastness that surrounded them.

A sound of desolate weeping filled the cavern and it caused Gairynzvl to cover his face with his hands, both in the pitch darkness of the nightmare and the diffuse light of the Healing Ward. Mardan stepped closer to his bedside, watching him with a potent combination of concern and confusion. Evondair placed both his hands upon Ayla's in a better attempt to discern the root cause of the nightmare.

Within the deepest recesses of his mind Gairynzvl could hear the same sound of desolate weeping that echoed around them, but it was not the childfey huddling close to them. The sound he heard was the recollection of his own crying as a youngling. The memory mingled with the sounds surrounding them with agonizing clarity and the taste of salt tears filled his mouth.

"Cut off his wing, you sniveling brat, or I'll throw you back to the legion!" A guttural voice pierced the shadows and caused them to flinch violently in revulsion. It was not an actual voice, but another memory hurled at them by those standing in the shadows.

"Why will she not waken?" Mardan asked with desperation filling his voice as he returned to Ayla's bed, distressed by her thrashings and sorrowful cries. Turning to gaze uncertainly first at Mardan and then at Gairynzvl, Evondair shook his head before he called loudly to the nearest Guard standing just outside the door.

"Awaken Veryth and bring him at once!"

A mournful wail serrated the darkness that wrenched at his heart and Gairynzvl could not fight his tears any more than he could prevent further images from filling his thoughts. With Ayla clinging to him and crying as bitterly as those around them, he closed his eyes tightly and tried to block the ghastly memories filling his mind. They were recollections that were not his own, but they were as clear as anything he could remember. Devastating imagery and sensations pummeled into him from the younglings gathered around them and, through him, they were communicated to her. Memories of blades and blood and screams tore at his self-control. Thoughts filled his mind of being forced to hurt and mutilate others as well as an inescapable fear of suffering the same if any measure of resistance was taken. It shook him to the core. Sensations of deprivation and isolation, of confusion and terror chilled Gairynzvl with their icy touch and, worst of all, images of the depravity that was forced upon the childfey made him shudder and growl in revulsion. Anguish and fury welled up inside him until he could no longer contain it.

Screaming into the blackness, the sound of his voice echoed in his ears, piercing the silence of the cavern along with the hush of the Healing Ward. Shaking himself fiercely into wakefulness, he pushed himself up from his reclining position and sat gasping for breath as he gazed around in horrified confusion. Tears fell unchecked from his eyes as he listened to the sound of Ayla's screams echoing his own and he could not control the violent shaking of his body.

Being closest to Ayla, Evondair instinctively encircled her in a comforting embrace and lowered his head to speak consoling words to her. Moving nearer to Gairynzvl with an expression of intense compassion and concern, Mardan reached out to lay his hand upon the Fierce One's trembling shoulder. Their gazes locked and, although they had both spoken words to each other in anger, the communication that passed between them at that moment required no articulation. Shaking intensely, Gairynzvl could not suppress his emotion and cried openly as he repeated over and again the only thought filling his mind.

"We must help them."

Chapter Fourteen

Although it took the remainder of the night, their tears finally abated and their violent trembling subsided, but the distressing memories could not be so easily dispelled. Such a nightmare was beyond ordinary and its significance had to be ascertained if anything beneficial could come from it. As the hours of the night expanded and then contracted Mardan paced nervously at the hearth, unwilling to sleep and unable to ignore his mounting concern. Evondair remained on duty despite the midnight hour having come and gone that signified the ending of his shift. During their vigil, Veryth spoke quietly with both of them.

Recounting the vision in its fullest measure was a task far more painful than either of them anticipated, but the imagery, the memories, and the voices contained within the harrowing nightmare held the key to unlocking its meaning. If its significance could be unraveled they could put it to use. Because Ayla had much greater difficulty dealing with the emotional turmoil the nightmare had hurled upon them than Gairynzvl encountered, Veryth decided not to separate them. Instead he asked them numerous questions and wrote many notes during their conversation, although he hesitated to formulate any opinions or offer explanations for the violent and disturbing dream they had experienced before he could speak with the Elders. Instead, he listened patiently, probed gently when tears and anger overruled logic, and ultimately concluded their discussion when Ayla's exhaustion made it impossible for her to concentrate.

Dawn was upon them. The night had slipped beyond their grasp. Since neither of them felt any desire to return to their bed or the unsettling prospect of sleeping, Veryth suggested they took some breakfast. After which they returned to their friends in the Healing Ward who waited for them with anxious concern. He encouraged them to share their experience as he felt certain the meaning of the vision would impact them all. Leaving them in the care of their friends and the attendant Healers, Veryth then went in the direction of the Devotionary with single minded purpose.

As the light of morning awakened the Temple inhabitants and the echoes of the Celebrant's daybreak chanting drifted softly throughout the halls and corridors of the complex, Gairynzvl stood silently before the window. Gazing outward without taking any notice of the illumination spreading from the horizon, he sighed deeply several times. His lavender-ice stare was red from much crying and restrained emotion. His body was weak with fatigue and his heart ached in a manner he had never known previously. He felt the warmth of the morning sun wash over him, but it did little to warm him. He was cold. His thoughts swirled in a dizzying haze of half seen memories that were not his own and the clouded recollections of his own past. He tried to fight them, but he felt powerless to combat the images that haunted him. They were a constant reminder of the pain he had suffered and the misery the childfey still trapped in the darkness of the Uunglarda bore every day.

Outside, a shimmering blanket of deep snow and glazings of sparkling ice graced the forest and the Temple complex, reflecting and refracting the light of morning into an incandescent glitter that caused him to close his eyes repeatedly and, finally, to turn away. Watching him from a far corner where the brilliant glow failed to reach her, Ilys frowned. In spite of fact that she never spoke about them, she could not deny her feelings for him any more than she could beguile herself into believing that he still felt as she did. She watched as he wandered the ward aimlessly, oblivious all of them except Ayla whom he gazed at repeatedly, though he did not approach her. Like him, she sat preoccupied by her thoughts as well as the emotion she could not oppose that left her frequently crying or shaking. It was this calamitous state of being that kept him from joining her.

Nayina sat by her side, speaking quietly and asking questions that were clearly far too painful for her to answer, although she made repeated attempts through much weeping. Their voices were soft, but Gairynzvl could hear them plainly through the transference of her thoughts and was unable to bear her despondency, mainly because it reminded him far too keenly of his own. Taken by a sudden rush of frustration with her sentimentality, he turned to scowl at her fiercely and hissed her name harshly, but his anger only served to weaken her further and Nayina glared at him as she gathered her friend into a protective embrace.

Getting up from the place near the hearth where he sat meditatively, Mardan fixed his wings with resolute purpose and moved towards him. Yet even as he walked nearer, Gairynzvl turned aside. Unable to bear the thought of another quarrel with the quick-tempered Celebrant, he tried to contain the reaction of hostility mounting within him, but he was unprepared when Mardan reached him and stood wordlessly for a moment before speaking.

"She cannot help it and you know that," Mardan reminded him unaccusingly, tempering his own annoyance over her emotional frailty with as much insight as he could manage. Moving closer to speak more confidentially, he then lowered his voice to nearly a whisper. "I cannot comfort her. She will not allow me close to her in the shadows and confusion that have enveloped her. It would seem that *you* are the only one, at present, who can." He did not realize what he was saying, but his words rang in Gairynzvl's thoughts as the Elder's questions, put to him just days before, resounded in his thoughts.

Will you share your strength of purpose, your tenacity and resilience with her when there are only shadows of confusion? Will you comfort her even when there is no comfort to be found?

Returning Mardan's piercing gaze, he shook his head subtly and spoke in an equally soft tone so that only he could hear. "It was not my intention to steal her from you. Please know that. I only wanted her help."

His unforeseen apology caused Mardan to frown, but he shook his head as well, unable to find the appropriate words to express his thoughts. Gairynzvl avoided the uneasiness of further emotion, however, by shifting the course of their conversation with intentional abruptness. "I want to go to Veryn Falls in search of Rehstaed. I think he would be a powerful ally and I hope to recruit him to help us."

Mardan stared at him with visible concern, but did not immediately argue with him and Gairynzvl continued hurriedly.

"Would you consider leading me to his cottage?" His question not only surprised Mardan, but Reydan as well who sat only a few yards away attempting not to overhear their conversation in the hush of the Healing Ward. Getting up from his place, he moved closer to them with unmistakable curiosity.

"You may be disappointed," he began without preamble. "Rehstaed has only one interest these days and it is generally crimson hued,"

Mardan nodded in agreement with this observation and continued by pointing out the obvious. "You will need more than one Guard at your side to breech the gates of The Uunglarda and keep Ayla and the childfey safe." To his amazement, Gairynzvl agreed.

"I would not volunteer anyone to accept such risks as entering The Uunglarda poses, but I cannot protect them on my own. The only ones I can ask stand round me, with the exception of Rehstaed who may or may not choose to offer help to another over drowning himself in wine, but I must ask."

Looking at each other quizzically, neither Mardan nor Reydan had opportunity to speak further before their conversation was interrupted by Bryth, who had come in search of his new friend when the news of the nightmare he and Ayla had shared spread through the ranks of the Temple Guard. "Why must you ask him?" His blunt question turned heads from every corner of the room, but he asked what each of them quietly wondered.

Without faltering, Gairynzvl turned to face the tall Fey Guard and answered in a voice loud enough for all those around him to hear. "Rehstaed had something irreplaceable stolen from him. He dwells in shadows even though he lives in the Light. I know precisely what that feels like and, although I cannot say with certainty, perhaps through helping others he may find some measure of peace for himself." The astuteness of what he said surprised them all, save one, who already knew the depths of his compassion in spite of his outward severity and the life he had been forced to lead as a Dark Fey. Gazing up at him affectionately, Ayla smiled and wiped the tears from her face as she listened to the gentle apology he whispered to her through the soft touch of his thoughts.

Unreservedly agreeing, Bryth and the other malefey offered to join him in his visit to Rehstaed's unassuming home, certain their presence at his side would help to persuade the determinedly standoffish Fey, but before they could make any further plans Veryth returned. Listening to their conversation, he added his support and explained that the Elders wished to meet with Gairynzvl, Ayla and any who wished to join them in their endeavor at the setting of the sun that day. Prompted by this news, the malefey gathered coats and cloaks and took their leave.

The bluster of cold that greeted them was not nearly as enlivening as flying free above the forest of his home for the first time in over fifteen years. Following the others, Gairynzvl found his attention wavering, captured by the beauty of the woodland that stretched out beneath them dressed in its winter robes.

Standing In Shadows

Garments of snow and ice glittered in the new day's sunlight. The deep snow lent a hush and stillness to the forest that, during other seasons, rang with the songs of birds and the air was cleaner and smelled sweeter than he ever could have remembered.

Veryn Falls was surprisingly close to the Temple complex and, even clasped in winter's bleak embrace, the waterfall cascaded and tumbled from the heights of the Ryvyn Mountains. Its splashing plunge was blunted and muffled by outcroppings of rock that were coated in thick layers of ice and hoarfrost and the deep pool at its base, emeraldine in the depths of summer, was obscured entirely from view by snow. Around the falls, a clearing stretched outward that was broad and filled with lacewings by summer though now it lay silent and still beneath a lush blanket of white.

Mardan smiled inwardly as they passed over the clearing, recalling the first hours he had spent with Ayla in that peaceful place and the contentment of those magical early days. For a moment, resentment filled his heart and he glanced over his shoulder at Gairynzvl, but he could not maintain his hateful thoughts. It was not because he had unpredictably apologized and it was certainly not because he was irresistibly congenial, but there was something about the Dark One, something he never anticipated, but could no longer deny. It was something he could not hate even if he often wished to.

Reydan righted himself in the air and pointed downward at a small cote situated upon the gentle slopes of the Ryvyn Mountains where it was protected from the threatening gales of winter and warmed by the sun. Inconspicuous and barely worth noticing, it boasted little more than a smoking chimney and several casks upon its porch, which were presumably empty. Gazing at each other incredulously, they descended to the yard and trudged through the nearly knee deep snow the final few feet that led up to the porch.

Bryth stepped back and bowed ceremoniously, motioning Gairynzvl to the door with exaggerated deference and the others smiled at his jest, certain they were wasting their time. Drawing a deep breath, Gairynzvl kicked the snow from his boots and stepped up onto the porch while glaring sideward at Bryth for his unspoken taunting. Pausing at the door, he raised his hand to knock and then cocked his head to one side and listened intently through the oaken portal for any sounds emanating from the interior. Nothing could be heard.

Setting his wings in a bold posture, Gairynzvl closed his fist and knocked upon the door, certain the hour was still too early to find the object of their search awake. He was not proven incorrect. Silence answered. Looking back at the others uncertainly, Gairynzvl sought their council and received nods and gestures encouraging him to try again. He did so, turning his fist to the side to bang against the thick oaken door as hard as the cold would permit; still, only quietness answered. Bryth glanced over his shoulder at Mardan, an unsurprised expression flickering in his gaze, but the Celebrant scowled and stepped up onto the porch to move to the entranceway purposefully. Once there, he kicked the snow from his boots against the heavy door frame repeatedly, making as much noise as he could manage and nodding resolutely at Gairynzvl who could not keep from laughing at his audacity.

At last, a sound was heard from within. It was an impudent response to the clatter they were making in a language he did not recognize, although when he heard it, Bryth's smile widened. Moving closer to the door as well, he too kicked the heavy portal and shouted back to the one inside in the same beguiling language. Reydan laughed heartily at the scene and joined in by wrapping upon the window while Gairynzvl stood back and watch them with amazed laughed, but their brashness was effective. After many moments of creating an increasing crescendo of noise, the door swung open to reveal Rehstaed who was dressed in nothing but a pair of disheveled sleeping trousers and a pair of warm woolen socks. He held a massive sword in his hands.

"Wha' in th' name o' all th' Ancients!" he shouted over the din they were making, his peculiar accent marking each word. Laughing and smiling inoffensively, the malefey desisted and stood back to enjoy his obvious astonishment when he realized who they were. "By th' Elders! Bryth! Mardan? Well call me a coquettish shefey for cursin' you to th' depths o' th' Uunglarda! Wha' brings you 'ere on such a morn, an' at such an unseemly hour?"

As if by one consent, the malefey turned to look at Gairynzvl, gesturing at him with open hands and bowing low as if to introduce a sovereign from some distant realm. Gairynzvl smiled broadly and stepped forward, speaking in a deep tone that filled the hush left when the others ceased their noisemaking. "The depths of The Uunglarda, in fact."

"And the hour is hardly unseemly, though your lack of apparel certainly is!" Bryth added in a jeering manner while Rehstaed lowered his sword and stepped backward into the warmth of the cottage. Gsturing at them to hurry inside as well so he could close the door, he defended himself with a scowl that would have made even the most fearsome Dark Fey pause. Rehstaed then noted that he could not be held responsible for his attire, or the lack thereof, when he was awakened so inhospitably by a raucous clamor that would have awakened the Ancients themselves if he had allowed it to continue. They enjoyed his mirth, as well as the warmth of the fire radiantly blazing beneath the hearth as he collected more appropriate garb. After Bryth assisted in lacing his shirt round his wings, he sat down at the table to inquire more specifically why they had chosen to visit him.

"You speak o' th' Uunglarda. Why?"

Sitting down across from him, Gairynzvl explained his reasons thoroughly, briefly sharing the tragedy of his history. He focused upon the realities of The Uunglarda and the horrors faced each day by all who were forced to live there, but most importantly by the childfey, whom he wished to liberate. Repeating much of what he had already shared with those now standing round him, he was also careful to point out that The Elders supported his plan and included the fact that they were to meet with them in the evening to discuss the final details of their strategy.

Listening quietly, Rehstaed neither showed support nor disparagement for what he heard. Rather, he allowed the newly Prevailed Dark One to speak his mind and communicate all he had to share. After hearing him out, he sat back and looked at those who stood around Gairynzvl, quietly supporting him. He took time to gaze long at each one of them before he stood and moved towards Reydan. "You are a musician," he noted skeptically.

Reydan nodded. "I am, and I know little of weaponry or fighting, but I cannot stand idle knowing what these little ones suffer," he explained resolutely. "I would rather die trying to rescue just one than live the remainder of my days knowing I did nothing when I had the chance to make a difference."

Gazing back at him fixedly, Rehstaed's violet eyes seemed to pierce him to his core, seeking the truth of what he said without asking anything further and Reydan did not oppose his unspoken quest, fully aware of his particular gift of discernment. Satisfied, Rehstaed moved to Bryth. "You encourage this madness?" He knew just how to speak to the born warrior, having served with him many times and familiar with his cavalier manner. Keenly aware of Gairynzvl's glare at such an observation, Rehstaed gazed contemplatively at the Fey Guard before him, but he received a smile in answer.

"You may quest as you wish, Discerning One, but you shall find no hesitation here," Bryth answered purposefully. He had learned the details of Gairynzvl's plan at the same time Rehstaed had, but willingly opened himself to the other's reading. Rehstaed shook his head.

"I need no' read you, my friend. I see plain as plain you are ready t' die for this one's purpose an' if you feel so strongly, knowin' him so little, *I* canno' doubt him." Having said this, Rehstaed turned his gaze to Mardan and moved closer to him with a glint in his violet eyes he could not hide. "An' if e'en Mardan is ready t' follow a Dark One back into th' Uunglarda, then I am ready t' join you as well." He chose his words wisely. Having quickly discerned the Celebrant's uncertainty about the endeavor, he tested his resolve with his carefully chosen words and he was not disappointed by his cunning duplicity. Shaking his head slowly, Mardan stepped back from him with a frown.

"I am a Celebrant. What aid could I offer in The Uunglarda?" His tone betrayed his misgivings yet, even as Rehstaed nodded concurringly and turned away, Bryth stepped closer to him.

"We all know the heart of a true warrior beats within your chest, Mardan. Why do you continue to deny it?" His query caused Mardan to flinch and step back once again, although inwardly he could find no means of contradicting what the Fey Guard said. Gairynzvl got to his feet and moved closer to the Celebrant as well.

"You are as fierce a warrior as any I have ever faced and we would be fortunate to have you beside us in the dark of The Uunglarda."

Shaking his head, Mardan could not accept the truth of what they said, even if it made perfect sense to him.

"He 'as no stomach for warfare. Why d' you harass him so?" Rehstaed turned, voicing his opposition to their attempts to persuade the reluctant Celebrant and choosing his next words even more carefully. "He was born for leadin' prayer an' incantations, no' blood an' battle an' death. Leave him be."

"I agree, my friend, he is a born leader, but not for praying and chanting," Bryth insisted determinedly and Reydan could not disagree.

"Forgive me, Mardan. I know you feel strongly about following the dedication your parents prepared for you, but surely you realize your temperament is not suited to the serenity of a Celebrant."

Growing vexed by their persistence, Mardan glared at them crossly. He had studied many years to fulfill the dedication his parents had planned for him and, in spite of the fact that he felt far more comfortable among those friends he had of the Fey Guard than any of the Celebrants he had come to know, he shook his head, unwilling to agree they were right. "I am a Celebrant. It is already decided. I cannot change that."

Chapter Fifteen

The wide doors to the Temple Devotionary swung open slowly, pulled back by two Fey Guards Gairynzvl recognized from Team Thunder. As he passed, they gazed at him with openly curious expressions. Equally familiar with him from the game they enjoyed the previous night, they did not understand why the Elders would be meeting with him at such a principal hour. It was now the hour of the setting sun when Light diminished and magic was said to take flight, but he did not engage either of them in conversation, nor did Bryth, who stood beside the Fierce One with an air of determination and focus they knew better than to question. As the doors opened, the glowing light of the Devotionary poured out into the dim hallway, enveloping each of those waiting in a spectral radiance that seemed to hold special significance.

Waiting for Gairynzvl to lead them inward, no one moved until he stepped tentatively forward. Following Veryth who waited just within the vast hall, they moved towards the dais where the Elders sat quietly meditating and awaiting their arrival. Without opening their eyes to gaze upon those who had entered, they nodded in agreement with those present. Their powerful thoughts were clearly perceived by the Fierce One who stood before them, but they were cognizant of the fact that not all of them shared his gift of telepathy and the youngest of the Three stood. Opening his pale cerulean eyes, he spoke in a steady tone, repeating the Prophecy of Reclamation that foretold the coming of The One who walks in Light and Shadow.

"*Out of the Darkness, Light shall burst forth, Indomitable. And the Light will Prevail over the Darkness by shining into it, Unwavering; Guiding the Innocent from shadow and the irresolute from placidity.*"

Those standing round listened with surprise as the ancient prophecy was spoken and even Ayla shook her head with amazement at hearing the words another time, still astonished that neither she nor Mardan, who had studied the ancient texts for so many years, had realized the impact it would have upon their lives. She looked behind her, sensing his presence in the dim corridor just beyond the Devotionary doors although he had not joined them when they left the Nursing Ward to make their way to the Devotionary. Wondering quietly what he would do, she did not interrupt the young Elder when he continued.

"Gairynzvl, son of Light and Sorrow, you stand ready to face certain peril in the cause of Reclamation with these few comrades at your side. Are there any others upon whom you wait?" Turning to gaze around him, Gairynzvl frowned when he did not find Mardan standing with them, but shook his head.

"Those who are willing are here." His reluctant reply was met with silence and the Third did not continue. Instead, he looked towards the open portal with patient expectation and his gaze was answered by a voice from the hallway.

"Not all."

Turning around again, Gairynzvl was astonished to see the Healer, Evondair, standing undecidedly in the doorway with Mardan lingering in the shadows just behind him. Veryth smiled and bowed subtly, gestured for them to enter, ushering them forward while nodding approvingly, though he did not speak. The youthful Elder nodded as well, as if he had made such a query with the full knowledge that they hesitated just beyond sight. Evondair moved into the chamber and stood beside Bryth, the hood of his robe pulled back in order to be seen more clearly. The golden sheen of his blond hair and brilliant white of his expansive wings reflected the flickering light in the room. Behind him, Mardan walked into the bright chamber more indecisively, speaking without preamble with at tone that was unmistakably irresolute.

"Do you say that he is the One about whom the prophecy speaks?" His forthright question brought nods from the other Elders, but it was the Third who responded, albeit somewhat cryptically.

"Do not you?"

Mardan frowned as the others who were gathered close to Gairynzvl turned to gaze at him. Shaking his head, he responded uncertainly. "I had not considered the possibility."

Smiling at this evidence of his confrontational nature, which he could not suppress even in the presence of the Three, the youthful Elder quipped a blunt reply. "Perhaps you should."

At this remark, the Second Elder stood and stepped forward. Collecting a suit of golden armor from a nearby table, he handed the traditional uniform of the Fey Guard to Mardan who accepted it without speaking. He stood gazing at it with consternation as the Second then repeated another prophecy that left them gaping at each other in dumbstruck silence.

"The Celebrant shall put aside his contemplations to don Golden Armor. The musician shall lay down his lute and take up a shield. The Healer shall relinquish his books to draw a sword and they shall defend Shadow amidst the darkness."

Then the First rose to his feet and stepped forward, moving down the steps of the dais to stand directly in front of Gairynzvl. Without speaking, he reached forward and laid his hand upon the crown of his head. The contact of the powerful Fey causing him to instantly close his eyes and groan in an effort to remain standing as the Elder sought answers to questions he would not articulate. In that moment, Gairynzvl heard his voice within his mind and through her nearness and unprepared state, so, too, did Ayla. Fully cognizant of her telepathic connection, the Elder wordlessly inquired about the nightmare they had shared. He did not desire a verbal reply, but rather, read their joint memory of the event as an answer.

Opening himself to the Elder, Gairynzvl unleashed the horror of the nightmare through his thoughts, permitting its terrifying imagery to flood back over both of them, as well as the strange sensations he had experienced the evening prior: sensations of being trapped, of being watched and of panic that had descended upon him for no reason whatsoever. At the touch of these appalling images and horrifying emotions the Elder gasped sharply, but he did not draw back. Ayla wavered at the combined potency of his intense telepathy and the harrowing repetition of the nightmare, her weakness drawing the support of Veryth, who was closest. He caught her before she collapsed to the floor. Then, the cries of childfey echoed from the shadows of their memory and upon hearing their wailing and experiencing the sensations of dread and misery that stemmed from the deepest roots of the nightmare, all Three Elders bowed their heads and keened unexpectedly in distress.

The sound was heart wrenching, as if they vocalized the full scope of sorrow, fear, pain and desolation they felt through the combination of the nightmare and Gairynzvl's own memories of The Integration. Not one Fey who stood within the precincts of the Devotionary could hear the sound without stopping and bowing their heads in dismay. Outside in the corridor, there was an unanticipated shuffling and whispers from the Guards as one they never expected to see inside the Temple stepped out of the dimness of the corridor into the glittering light of the Devotionary. He wore a hood pulled up over his head, but the bronze coloration of his wings betrayed his identity as he moved with a purposeful stride into the hall and he did not stop until he came to stand beside Gairynzvl.

"This is th' sound my heart made on th' day my wife an' child were stolen from me."

Gairynzvl turned to look at Rehstaed with an indistinguishable expression, but the Fey continued before he could find any means of responding. "This is th' sound my heart makes each an' every day."

The Elders drew a simultaneous breath, silencing themselves in order to listen more attentively to the one now speaking and the vast Temple complex seemed, somehow, utterly bereft in the absence of their voices.

"An' this is th' reason I've come; because I canno' bear th' sound any longer an' if my presence in your courageous band o' liberators can make any difference whatsoe'er, can stop this sound from smotherin' me, an' per'aps another soul as well, then 'ere I am." The unusual accent of his words and foreign inflection gave his identity away to those who stood round, yet Gairynzvl only nodded grimly, in perfect agreement with every word he spoke. Turning back to face the Elders, he spoke with a tone of finality.

"All are now here."

At this pronouncement, the Elders drew them closer, putting aside formality to discuss in far greater detail the particulars of Gairynzvl's plan. They added their own astute suggestions and explained that his increased telepathic and empathic sensitivity, which was made manifest through the nightmare he and Ayla shared, was also foretold in the ancient texts. They had been awaiting the confirmation of this final sign during their meditations and the nightmare that had shaken all of them so intensely had solidified their belief that he was the One spoken of in the Prophecy of Reclamation. The ancient writings indicated that this gift would blossom into its fullest degree in order to aid him in the search for the innocents he sought. However, they were also careful to warn him that this new awareness might compel him to make uncharacteristic decisions.

Briefly turning their attention to Ayla, they questioned her as to her own abilities and if she felt prepared to adequately protect herself in the domain of demons? She agreed that she could, but Ilys, who had up until this point stood silent and said nothing, shook her head. "She cannot control the emotions she senses and her unpredictability will not only hinder us, but could put us all in danger. She should stay behind." Shocked at her blatant objections, Ayla's friends attempted to argue in her defense, but she turned to direct her concerns to Gairynzvl alone. "You know well enough how easily the Hunters can detect the hidden. They will sense her emotional turmoil at once and give us away, whether or not I am able to bend light."

He shook his head. "We need her. She is The Guardian."

"She may well be, but she cannot control her empathy. It will devastate her in the Uunglarda and immobilize us."

The Elders watched and listened without interrupting as their disagreement became more heated and Ilys continued to point out Ayla's failings and weaknesses. "All I have ever seen her do is cry. How can that possibly aid us?"

Gairynzvl stepped closer to the Dark shefey, flexing his wings with clear agitation. "Only she can find the chilfey in the shadows and darkness. Only she will be able to hear their voices through the blackness."

Ilys shook her head aggressively, her silvery horns glinting and reflecting the light. "The Elders have just told you that your own gifts will serve that purpose. I tell you, we do not need her."

Moving closer still, Gairynzvl glared down into her upturned face with a menacing expression. "I will be far too busy finding the hidden avenues and opening and closing portals to be listening for the weeping of childfey," he snarled through clenched teeth, but she shook her head once again and turned to gesture at Ayla who stood listening to their argument with an agape expression of astonishment.

"She is going to cry even now. If she cannot bear the antagonism of two Fey, how will she possibly tolerate the animosity and resentment pouring down on her from thousands?"

He looked past Ilys at Ayla. In his heart he knew she was probably right, but he needed to hear Ayla say she was unable. To his surprise, however, her expression shifted. Her amber gaze narrowed as she drew her wings back with determination and strode closer to the Dark shefey who was not only taller than she was, but far more threatening. Placing her hands upon her hips, she drew a steadying breath and spoke with a tone of resolve that shocked them all. "I am a Guardian of Child Fey, trained by the Elders themselves and dedicated to a life of service and protection of the innocent. I may express my emotions freely and, perhaps, am at times overwhelmed by the emotions of others, but I am entirely capable of suppressing my sensitivity in order to protect myself and those around me, when it is necessary."

Ilys stared back at her, unconvinced. "Are you certain?"

Ayla moved closer to her and the intensity of her abrupt shift in temperament made even Gairynzvl step back from her in amazement. "No." Her answer shocked them all, but she continued undeterred. "None of us here can be certain how we will react in the darkness of the Uunglarda, but our strength lies with each other. By trusting each other we shall all be stronger through our unity and our confidence and reliance upon each other." Silence answered her words and in that hush, the Elders nodded harmoniously.

Ilys smiled shrewdly. "If you say so."

Chapter Sixteen

The chamber in which they stood was dim and sparsely furnished with only a small table placed near the door upon which a single candle stood. There were no windows in this room, which was unusual in a temple where Light was revered, but the purpose of this particular space required darkness. Having just entered, they stood gazing at the only other furnishing of the room in silence, astonished beyond speaking by the massive mirror standing centrally in the room. Its frame was made of darkly painted, unembellished wood, as was its heavy base and the broad supports that held it upright. Its glass reflected only the light filtering into the room from the torches in the corridor and the candle at the doorway, but this small amount of illumination was enough to keep the portal closed to crossing.

The fact that such a mirror even existed within the precincts of the Temple left them marveling, but the heavy layer of dust coating the frame and floor of the dim chamber betrayed the length of time that had passed since it was used. The complex locks upon the heavy, double doors, as well as the many spells of protection that guarded these doors and the permanent stationing of two Fey Guards outside the doors spoke volumes as well. If at any time while the massive mirror stood in darkness the Reviled attempted a crossing, they would find merely a vacant room from which there was no escape.

Taking up the candle from the door-side table, Veryth moved confidently into the room, gesturing wordlessly for them to accompany him and the small band of Liberators followed in mute curiosity. Gairynzvl went first, eager to be acting upon his plan at last, with Ayla close beside him. Mardan followed her closely, as did Nayina and Reydan, with Rehstaed, Bryth, Evondair and Ilys behind them. Each wore dark colored clothing that was warm and layered for protection against the seeking chill of the Uunglard and it was now that the leather and suede of Gairynzvl's outfit, fashioned by the Temple artisans, finally made sense. Rehstaed and Bryth wore the glimmering gold armor of the Fey Guard, as did Mardan. Each also carried a backpack containing tools they might need, a small bottle of Quiroth to fortify their strength, a small bundle of food consisting of a few apples, a small block of cheese and a dense bread made from hearty grains and seeds. A woolen cloak was rolled and secured at the top of the pack and from one side hung a length of rope. Additionally, all the malefey carried weaponry that would serve to protect them against the Reviled.

Gathering in front of the mirror, their uneasiness became more evident and Veryth turned to face them with a far more somber expression than that which typically favored his handsome features. Reaching for Gairynzvl, he drew him forward to stand before him and placed both hands upon his shoulders while he gazed deep into his liquescent eyes. "None present, with the exception of yourself and Ilys, have ever experienced a crossing before. They may find themselves disoriented and may need time to regain possession of their senses once you reach the other side."

Gairynzvl nodded his understanding, but said nothing. Veryth continued with an even tone, "This crossing-place will lead you to a quiet environ where you should be safe temporarily."

Gairynzvl nodded again, then turned to gaze back at Ayla with an expression of such intensity that none, including Veryth, interrupted him. "The Uunglarda is harsh, filled with misery and despair. You must protect yourself at all costs. You must block as much of the emotion you will encounter there as you are able to until I find the childfey. Only then, Ayla; only then, should you reach out to discern their natures. Will you be able to do this?" The authoritative edge to his deep voice left no room for debate and she only nodded, the concurrence of her thoughts expressing her full agreement. She knew he was correct, that she could not risk opening herself to the horrors of that bleak realm until the precise moment when her gift was required.

Satisfied that they were prepared, Veryth raised his hands from his shoulders and looked over him at the others. "I cannot follow you into the darkness, but will await your return at the designated place with Healers and Guards to aid you upon your return. You have had your differences and, without doubt, you shall have more in the taxing hours that here shall follow, but you must put your trust in Gairynzvl now. He will guide you in the shadows and lead you out into the Light once again."

Only a few deeply drawn breaths answered him, but the fair Healer smiled encouragingly and stepped away from the darkling portal the mirror presented. "I shall extinguish the candle and return to the corridor. Only when you hear that the locks upon the doors are in place should you endeavor to open the crossing."

Gairynzvl agreed that he would wait and, in preparation, the malefey around him drew their swords, but he quickly admonished their actions. "You will become dizzy and may find yourself feeling ill from using the portal. It is not advisable to have any weaponry unsheathed as you cross. It may injure you or another."

Mardan shook his head, instantly wary. "If we cross and the Reviled are waiting for us, should we not be prepared for battle?"

Beside him, Bryth also agreed, but their new leader shook his head resolutely, assuring them that it was far more dangerous to cross with blades unsheathed than to arrive at the other side without them in hand. "Each one must step through the portal on his own. We cannot go in pairs, but I will go through first to assure that the crossing-place is secure."

Bryth stepped forward with determination. "I shall follow to aid you if there are Dark Ones to be dealt with before the others cross."

Mardan stepped forward as well, insisting that he cross over next and that, for their own protection, the shefey should make their way last. All agreed and formed a line before the mirror. Veryth nodded and stepped outward into the entryway, gazing over them thoughtfully one final time and, although he was not a Celebrant, he spoke a blessing of protection for them before extinguishing the candle he held.

"Vrynnoth chae Luxonyth guildynn. May the Light that Guides you Vary Not." Then he left them standing in shadows as he closed and secured the doors to the Room of Transition. As dimness enveloped them, several of the friends drew unsteady breaths and Ayla could not help pressing close to Nayina with an instinctual dread of the darkness. In front of them, Ilys stifled a hiss of frustration at this evidence of her fear and turned to face the portal. Because her eyes were better suited to the darkness surrounding them she was able to watch with keen interest when Gairynzvl stepped closer to the portal and raised one hand before him, wielding a magic she did not possess.

"Hchrynoch drall enpach thrynnovich." His use of fluent Dlalth spawned more than a few shivers, as the guttural, defiled language was feared by the Fey of the Light even more greatly than darkness itself, but their trepidation quickly dissipated into curiosity when the mirror made a sound they never anticipated. Creaking like ice shifting on the shoulders of a frozen river, the dark glass of the mirror visibly warped in response to his words.

"Hchrynoch drynnovl enpackich thrynnul," Gairynzvl continued, altering the dark incantation he used in order to open the portal even further. Behind him, Mardan could not combat the shudder of revulsion that serrated through him, although he could not be sure whether this was in response to the gruesome language he was hearing or if it was an effect of opening the portal. Groaning more loudly in opposition to the spell being spoken, the mirror seemed to shift upon the floor. It seemed to twist on its base in an attempt to escape the abhorrent invocation while the ripples on its dark surface became more evident. Raising his other hand, Gairynzvl directed even more energy at the portal and increased the intensity of his tone as he spoke a third time.

"Hchrynoch thalinan drynnovl chi ennovat!" The mirror resounded with a thunderous sound, like that of rock splitting from the face of a cliff and shattering downward in a shower of debris, although not a single shard of glass broke from its face. Nevertheless, where there once had been a reflective plane, smooth and polished, a wavering surface like that of water slowly rose and fell before them. Turning to gaze back at those waiting upon his actions, he looked at them with an intense expression of determination.

"The portal is open. When you step over the threshold, do not stand still. Continue forward as if you were walking, regardless of how you may feel." Receiving grim nods in answer, he glanced briefly at Ayla and whispered gently to her through the soft touch of his thoughts before he turned to face the mirror. Drawing a deep breath, he savored the sweet, clean scent of the air around them, then he drew his wings tightly closed and stepped forward into the undulating face of the mirror.

His friends watched as he entered the gateway and was swallowed up by the dark, wavering surface of the mirror as he moved beyond it into another place. Having never actually witnessed a crossing before, the malefey watched with intense interest and glanced at each other with a palpable combination of anxiety and eagerness, while Ayla and Nayina gasped in dismay. Bryth waited for several hesitant moments, unsure how long it might take to cross and unwilling to make the attempt too soon and endanger his friend. When Ilys spoke in a hushed tone that he could go, he stepped forward, pulled his wings close as he had seen Gairynzvl do and drew a deep breath. Glancing behind him at Mardan only briefly with an expression that clearly betrayed his enthusiasm regardless of the inherent risk involved, he stepped forward into the undulating mirror.

Instantly a bizarre sensation washed over him that he could not control, a feeling like being slowly immersed into ice cold honey. The thick, heavy sensation enveloped him and drew him deeper within, pulling him while at the same time adhering to him in a suffocating embrace. Recalling the Fierce One's instructions to keep moving, Bryth stepped again into nothingness and felt as if he was falling, although the stifling murk surrounding him beguiled his vision so that he could no longer ascertain any direction. As the sucking, slurking darkness drew him deeper into its swirling center, for one terrifying moment, he lost awareness of his own body. Feeling as if he floated in the sodden darkness, it took all his concentration to take another step forward, but when he did he could hear the scrunch of gravel beneath his boots. Astonished by the sound emanating from out the deafening silence of the void, he looked downward. He was unable to see it, but the unmistakable sensation of solid ground beneath his feet re-collected his senses from the terrifyingly vacant euphoria into which they had momentarily slipped. The ability to step forward an additional time came easier with this reorientation and as he did the empty blackness seemed to release him and he slipped through it into a shadow-filled, sulfurous atmosphere.

Looking round him with immeasurable curiosity, Bryth located Gairynzvl standing a few feet away. He was gesturing to him to step forward again, away from the crossing-point, and with the first step the blank silence that had enshrouded him fell away. In the distance he could hear the incoherent muffled noises of countless souls in torment, wailing in distress or howling in pain. Insidious laughter twisted in the dingy dimness mingling with angry voices shouting in vulgar Dlalth. Moving closer to Gairynzvl with a grimace of disgust, Bryth's first query was not about the crossing or the odd sensations he experienced while inside the vortex. Instead he very bluntly inquired what the source of the horrid smell was that assaulted them.

Shaking his head with a wry smile, Gairynzvl responded with an ironic chuckle. "Welcome to the Uunglarda." As he spoke, Mardan stepped from the warping vortex and stumbled forward, half falling, half turning in complete disorientation. Somehow he managed to keep his feet under him in spite of the loose gravel underfoot that caused him to slide until he came to a stop next to Bryth. Straightening to gaze round him with a fierce scowl, he drew a shallow breath and snorted outward in revulsion. His friends wordlessly agreed with his unspoken assessment. Drawing him further from the portal for his own protection while he shook his head repeatedly in an attempt to clear the dizzying, whirling impression that lingered round him, they watched the place where he had just come from as it warped and rippled vigorously.

Rehstaed tumbled out of the portal next, a chaos of wings and limbs and curses spoken in his native language. Bryth understood and concurred with a dry chuckle even as he stepped forward to collect his disoriented friend. As the remainder of the Liberators crossed, Gairynzvl made a hasty reconnaissance of the area to ensure there were no Legionnaires loitering in the shadows, but they were, as Veryth had assured them, temporarily safe.

When all had crossed, he returned to the huddled group and moved directly to Ayla to take her hands in his own. Although he did not verbally speak to her, their gazes locked and their wings moved in spontaneous union as she nodded and closed her eyes with a wan smile. Recognizing their telepathic communication instantly, Mardan scowled with resentment and turned aside to gaze around him at the bleak, inhospitable landscape rather than jeopardize their safety by hurling accusations upon the only one who could return them to Hwyndarin.

The terrain was desolate, filled with jagged outcroppings of rock that blocked the way and cavernous rifts in the ground that yawned vacuously, threatening to swallow up any unfortunate soul that might tumble into their depths. The ground itself was a dull, wasted gray in color. It was devoid of any form of life or life-giving nutrient. No trees or plants grew in the lifeless soil to cleanse the air and, as a result, the sky matched the soil's pallid color with little variation of hue. Filled with smoke and shadows that seemed to twist and writhe of their own accord, the air reeked of sulfur and the putrid stench of rot.

The place where they now stood was little more than a covert to one side of a dusty, meandering track. The barren roadway wound along a vast conglomerate of rocks that stretched away to one side of them and led to a squalid encampment several hundred yards in the opposite direction. Gairynzvl looked around them carefully, deliberating over the best course to take in order to reach the place he sought: the cave where partially integrated childfey were cloistered as punishment. Squinting into the smoky, dusty murk, he attempted to judge what side of the encampment lay closest to them, but his eyes were no longer suited to the dingy atmosphere and bleak light of the Uunglarda. This alteration forced him to turn and gaze at Ilys. "Do you recall this encampment?"

At hearing his uncertainty, Mardan closed his eyes in an attempt to hide his already piqued irritation. Rehstaed and Evondair glanced at each other with sudden doubt, but Ilys nodded, pointing towards the far side of the camp. "Golnathum Gorge is on the far side of the encampment."

Gairynzvl twisted about to peer into the distance once again, but shook his head and sighing sharply.

"What is the matter?" Mardan queried sharply, unable to disguise his annoyance and eager to set off before they could be discovered.

"Our goal lies on the opposite side of that camp," came Gairynzvl's exasperated reply. Returning to the group, he offered two possible routes for them to consider. "We can keep to this track and skirt round the camp. This will keep us further from the Reviled, but going around will take more time and this dust will betray our location and draw attention to us regardless of how well Ilys can bend light." To illustrate his meaning, he twisted round and kicked the parched gravel of the roadway, generating a cloud with little effort. "We could also cut straight through the center of town where the road is better paved and less likely to expose our passing, but we will need to rely upon our Light Bender to shield us."

Heads turned as the friends gazed at each other and uncertainly considered these choices, but Mardan offered a third option. "Or we could fly." He tersely stated as if the alternative seemed more than obvious, but both Gairynzvl and Ilys shook their heads at his suggestion.

"Look up," the former Dark One suggested with conspicuous patience. "The air is filled with sulfur and other toxins that would render you unconscious in moments. No one flies in the Uunglarda without a tox-guard and we do not have any."

Nodding with mute acceptance of this fact, the malefey drew closer to debate while Gairynzvl stepped back and waited, unwilling to force a decision upon them they might later resent. As they discussed the options before them, Ilys slipped away from the group unobserved and gazed fixedly into the nearby rocky outcropping. Bending her wings subtly, she shook her head, then turned to gaze at the encampment.

Chapter Seventeen

"We should go through town and we ought to go in two groups." Ilys stated matter-of-factly, coming back to the huddled friends and speaking with the same blatant self-assurance she had displayed when she first appeared to them. She did begrudgingly admit that she had never shielded so many and could not guarantee they would pass entirely undetected, but she suggested taking Gairynzvl and Ayla first, along with whichever Guard they chose who would see to their protection. She would leave them at the entrance of the Braying Caverns and then return for the others.

"Is that really what you call it?" Nayina cried, fully aware of the use of the terrible place, but unable to remain silent any longer as the heaviness of despair and the weight of the gloom around them pressed down on her.

Gairynzvl nodded and answered in a soft tone, "what happens within its walls is even more dreadful than the name suggests. You should prepare yourself for what you will see and hear."

Comprehending his warning she stood for a long moment and stared at him uncertainly. Shaking her head more and more fervently as she contemplated what terrifying sights she might see in such a place, she could not hold back the tears that suddenly overwhelmed her. Moving toward her friend, Ayla attempted to comfort her, but both Gairynzvl and Mardan shouted at her in unison.

"Do not reach out!"

Closest to her, Mardan grasped her arm tightly and pulled her back, resolutely checking her instinctual empathy before she could endanger herself or anyone else. "Nayina will be fine. I know it is your nature to empathize, but do *not* put yourself at risk, Ay."

Gazing up at him in surprise for his admonishment, she shook her head and drew her senses inward before they slipped into the dark void around them.

Softly she muttered an apology. "Sorry, I was not thinking." He nodded with understanding, but Ilys hissed under her breath and turned away.

"Well think next time. There are Legionnaires everywhere and we cannot have you losing control *here*."

No one opposed her outburst. Stifling her emotion, Nayina shook her head. "It is I who am sorry. I hoped I would be able to be of some assistance, to help with the little ones, but the thought of what happens to those poor childfey is too much. I cannot bear it. I should go back and wait for your return with Veryth." Her pronouncement surprised them, but Reydan stepped closer and drew her to him in a warming embrace, whispering his agreement with her decision and assuring her of his return. Ayla and Mardan moved nearer as well, sharing supportive words and hugs before Nayina turned back to the portal, but their display of patience and acceptance made Ilys roll her eyes. Turning to gaze in the direction of the encampment, she moved closer to Gairynzvl and reminded him to close the portal before they set off.

After he had done so, he took Ayla by the hand and drew her to the front of the group while looking fixedly at Mardan, inquiring if he would be accompanying them. Before he could answer, however, Evondair stepped forward unexpectedly, the sallow surroundings seeming to have no effect upon the bright glimmer of his golden hair or the resplendent whiteness of his wings, which stood out in sharp contrast to the dull, gray environment.

"With all respect to Mardan, you do not need another Guard at your side. If you are discovered by any Legionnaires either you or Ilys will be able to dispatch them, but when you find the childfey, you are far more likely to require the aid of a Healer." His logic was irrefutable and, although he was not skilled with weaponry or fighting, it was Evondair who joined the first group to attempt to reach the Braying Caverns. The remaining malefey would guard the portal and await Ilys' return. In agreement, Gairynzvl looked intently at each one of them and, though none possessed a gift of telepathy so that they might hear his thoughts, they nodded their understanding back to him before he turned away.

Setting off in a tight formation with Ilys in the lead, it did not take long for the murk of the Uunglarda to envelope them. Watching them disappear into the shadowy landscape, Mardan could not keep from growling under his breath, but when he could no longer see them he turned back to the portal and his friends waiting for him. Discussing their tactics, the malefey took up stations facing in each cardinal direction, although none of them could ascertain with certainty which direction was which in the bleary dimness sinking around them. Their course set, they would wait for Ilys to return and plan for the possibility that she would not.

Moving along the dusty track as quietly as they could manage, the four Fey walked lightly and stepped with diligence over the graying, chalky gravel of the roadway. Although it had appeared much farther away from their location near the portal, the encampment suddenly loomed out of the elusive gloom and echoes of cries of torment and lascivious laughter came from all corners. As they drew closer, Gairynzvl looked down at Ayla repeatedly, inquiring without speaking if she was able to block the piercing emotion pouring out of the encampment like a flood, which he could easily sense as a result of his own heightened awareness. Nodding mutely, she indicated her present stability without shifting her concentration. Gairynzvl then glanced behind him at Evondair. He knew he had the gift of discernment and wondered if he could also hear him, but, although the Healer returned his gaze with a penetrating stare, Gairynzvl did not hear his thoughts come back in answer to his wordless inquiry.

"Stop!" Ilys whispered harshly, drawing them close together as a triplet of Legionnaires lurched around a small outcropping of rocks just to the left of the track. She moved her hand over her head as if drawing a circle over them in the open air and the light briefly distorted around them. At the unexpected shimmer the Dark Ones paused to look about with obvious confusion. Ayla clamped a hand across her mouth to prevent herself from gasping out loud as fear latched onto her with icy fingers, but, standing as close as they were beneath the wrinkle of light Ilys had created, she could feel the warmth of the malefey who had moved on either side of her for protection. She did not need to stretch out her senses to feel the security of their strength encompassing her and the sickening sensation of dread that threatened to overpower her subsided.

Speaking in vulgar Dlalth, the three Reviled Ones tramped closer to their hiding place. They swayed with visible intoxication as they peered into the empty landscape before them and one leaned too far and nearly tumbled into his comrade beside him. They cursed at each other vehemently and shoved the wavering one away before they continued to quarrel amongst themselves.

Their dispute was heated and it was evident even to the two Fey of the Light who did not understand Dlalth, that they complained about some task they had been instructed to undertake, but did not want to. As the unsteady group staggered past, one stopped abruptly and turned aside, coming to within inches of Ilys who scowled at his repulsiveness and leaned as far back from him as she could possibly manage while he tugged his filth-laden trousers open and pissed on the ground at her feet while the others howled with loutish glee and continued down the track.

When they disappeared into the distance, Ilys cursed in equally appalling Dlalth and stamped away from the sodden puddle at her feet, kicking dust over her boots in an attempt to dry them. As she continued to grumble in disgusted Dlalth, Gairynzvl turned with Evondair to gaze after the inebriated triplet, realizing they were going in the direction of the portal and their friends. Turning back, they agreed they needed to hasten their pace and regrouped in a much closer formation than they had originally used as Ilys took up the lead once more. Reminding them to move as silently as possible and to remain as close together as they might manage so she could conceal them more effectively, she turned her hand over their heads once again. The shimmering light that encircled them reflected its surroundings rather than illuminating them and obscured them from view as they crossed the boundaries of the camp.

The reeking encampment hissed and groaned like a living creature, emitting sulfurous vapors that hung on the air so thickly they could been seen by the naked eye. The overwhelming stench caused them to catch hold of their breath until reaching less putrid surroundings, but there was not an inch of the camp that did not reek and ultimately the foul odor had to be breathed in. Ilys led them straight down the center of the main thoroughfare where few Dark Ones lingered and only the odd conveyance wheeled by them. Most of the Reviled huddled in clusters around sputtering open braziers, attempting to extract some meager warmth from their malodorous glimmers. As they passed silently by the tattered and overcrowded tents and poorly constructed buildings that were so old they were nearly falling down, Ayla could not keep from staring, taken aback by the shocking sights that assailed her from every direction.

On one side of the road a small group of Legionnaires were taking sport with a she-Demon in plain sight of any who might pass. On another corner several Legionnaires in shoddy uniforms were watching the goings-on across the street and shouting lewd suggestions while making bets upon the outcome.

The Liberators continued quietly down the street, passing a raucous brothel filled to bursting with so many of The Fallen they poured out onto the shabby porch and were lying in the gutters, half-dressed and unreservedly drunk. In her astonished distraction, Ayla was repeated jostled by the others when her lack of attention kept her from matching their hurried pace. Yet when they passed a black tent from which issued the unmistakable wails of a childfey in distress, both Gairynzvl as well as Evondair had to place their hands upon her shoulders to keep her moving forward.

"We cannot help him right now," Gairynzvl whispered sharply through his thoughts, although the intensity of his emotion betrayed his desire to slip into the tent under the protection of bent light and kill the offending Legionnaire before he could do any further harm. In that moment, with both their hands upon Ayla, Evondair felt the rage and revulsion churning within Gairynzvl and he, in turn, could hear the Healer's less than benevolent thoughts that did not differ all too greatly from his own. The malefey stared at each other in surprise at this discovery, realizing in that moment of intense emotion that Ayla was acting as a living conduit between them, but they had no time to respond in any further way. Ilys scowled in anger and quickened her pace in an attempt to put greater distance between them and the yowls of pain coming from the dark tent.

Unable to argue for fear of being left behind and discovered, the others followed her closely as she turned their rapid walk into a run. Their increased pace required even greater care in order to not kick up any dust from the roadway or generate any additional sounds that might betray their passage. Hastening their speed brought them to the far edge of the camp within moments, however, and as soon as they were safely surrounded by outcroppings of rock once again, Ilys stopped and retracted the bubble of light she had cast over them. Catching her breath rapidly, she turned to gaze back in the direction of the black tent and spoke in a low tone that Gairynzvl recognized only too well. "I could go back on my own and get him. None would see me." The determination in her voice was not to be contradicted, but Gairynzvl stepped closer.

"You promised to return for the others at the portal. They are probably already under attack by the Legionnaires who passed us sent to scout the perimeter of the encampment."

She shook her head. "I can take the childfey with me back to the portal and your friends. They can look after him until it is time to meet up with you."

Once again Evondair stepped forward. Unexpectedly, he added his voice to her argument, surprising both Ayla, who stood desperately trying to force back her tears, and Gairynzvl who had already begun to sense the pain of those childfey trapped within the confines of the Braying Caverns in the distance. The Healer's voice was calm, but imposing. "Is this not why we are here, to rescue younglings? If she is able to liberate him from his captivity and can do so without being seen and without putting our plans at risk, why should she not?"

Gairynzvl stared at him hesitantly, afraid that their entire plan might unravel right there, but he nodded and reached to take Ilys by the arm before she winked out of sight. "Do not abandon our friends. They are relying upon you." The demanding of his voice caused her to winced, but she turned her response into an affected laugh and patted him on the shoulder dramatically before she spun, waved her hand over her head and vanished.

Evondair watched the track behind them for any sign of her passing, listening keenly for the slightest footfall or scrunch of gravel beneath her boots, but only the distant chaos of the village reached his ears and he returned his attention to the task at hand. Gairynzvl had stepped several yards away from them and raised his hands to his ears to help capture the sounds he waited to hear, but only silence drifted upon the bleak, cold air. Moving closer to Ayla, Evondair gazed down at her with the judicious concern of a Healer as he attempted to discern her emotional stability, but she had dried her tears and shook her head. Smiling up at him dimly, he assured him that she was still in control without needing to speak.

Gairynzvl moved several yards further away, closing his eyes as he turned slowly in a circle and listened keenly with his perfectly pointed ears as well as his newly, highly-attuned senses. Although he had never done such a thing before, he stretched out his senses like a fisherman casting a net into deep waters and it felt oddly natural to him. All he touched, however, was the barren landscape. There were no signs of life or sounds emanating from the rocky hillsides. He had just sensed childfey and heard their sorrowful voices. Where had they gone? Why were they now utterly silent?

His companions watched with growing concern as long moments passed. Fearful of being discovered by some straggling Dark One and even more apprehensive about the possibility of not finding those whom they sought, they watched quietly. Ayla turned her head slightly to one side, considering something she had not before; then she stepped forward and reached for Gairynzvl's hands when he turned to stare at her with bewilderment.

"Let me help you," she spoke softly, fully aware of the danger involved in opening herself to the environment, but convinced it was what she needed to do. It was what she had done in their dream. Only half comprehending her suggestion, Gairynzvl reached for her slowly and when their hands touched a strange sensation washed over him. Instantly they sensed they were not alone, regardless of the fact that the dimness surrounding them in the failing light of evening was nearly impenetrable. Compelled to move forward into the gloom, Gairynzvl took a single step towards a low-lying ridge of rocks in the distance while she paused and reached out with her free hand, as if feeling for those waiting to be found. They closed their eyes together as a blurred vision of shades shifting in stifling darkness suddenly reared up in their minds. A feeling of being terrified and alone poured over them like a deluge of icy water. Suddenly, Gairynzvl felt surrounded and a suffocating fear descended upon him that made him gasp loudly and open his eyes with a start.

Pointing into the blackness in the direction of the ridge lying half obscured by murk and fog several hundred yards in the distance, he motioned for them to follow even as he began to run along the track. Evondair grasped Ayla by the hand as he passed her and tugged her along with him, but she could not contain a sob of bitter anguish as her thoughts touched absolute misery.

Chapter Eighteen

Darkness spiraled upon billows of smoke that swirled in the raucous clamor of the reeking encampment and shadows lurched within the thick bleakness. Through this writhing miasma, a barely perceptible shape moved along the main roadway travelling more rapidly than the ordinary onlooker might be able to follow and heading towards the only black tent in camp. No sounds came from this tent, not any longer, although the cries of a childfey had recently been heard echoing through the neighboring hovels and unkempt buildings lining the street. These sounds had caused many of the resident Dark Ones to withdraw to the farthest end of town or drink more fervently from the nearest bottle. This tent was known for its horrors. It was the Centurion's tent and he frequently took pleasure in causing pain.

Into the blackness of this tent the fleeting apparition floated unobserved and only the slightest movement of one of the tent flaps betrayed its presence. Within the rancid bivouac, Ilys paused to allow her eyes a moment to adjust to the darkness while she sought the youngling they had all heard only a few moments ago. The interior of the tent was littered with remnants of clothing, strewn about like sordid trophies. Empty bottles and grimy trenchers with half-eaten food lay heaped against one corner, the stench of mold and rot so heavy on the air that she raised a hand to cover her nose and mouth in an attempt to stifle a reflexive gag. Pressed up against the far side of the tent, the Centurion lay upon a cot lined with feathers plucked from his unfortunate victims. The noise of his prodigious snore pronounced his deeply unconscious state and this discovery brought a twisted grin to Ilys' lips.

Cowering in the opposite corner as far from the massive Dark One as her chains would permit, a small childfey perhaps eight years of age watched her captor with the terrified focus of a trapped animal. When Ilys saw her she froze instinctively, then moved closer and crouched down in front of the childling before she slowly moved her hand over her head, to retract the beguiling twist of light that concealed her. Instantly the childfey started backward in surprise, yet she did not make a sound as she stared with dismay at the she-Demon who had magically appeared before her eyes. Raising her finger to cover her lips in a gesture to keep quiet, Ilys smiled sweetly at the alarmed little one and shook her head before she leaned closer to whisper in a hushed tone. "I know you cannot trust me, but I promise I will not hurt you. I am here to help you."

The childfey gazed back at her in mute terror, although the glimmer of hope that sparkled in her emeraldine gaze was unmistakable. Turning to glance over her shoulder at the sleeping Centurion, Ilys canted her head in his direction. "I will show you that you can trust me." Standing cautiously, Ilys stepped nearer to the hulking Dark One who was rattling the tent with his gurgling snores. Stooping as she drew closer, she reached for a dagger that had been tossed to the floor and slunk closer. The childfey shuffled backwards with a choked gasp when she realized what the she-Demon was about to do.

Raising the blade high, Ilys smiled viciously as she prepared to sink the dagger into the Centurion's throat, but before she could achieve this the little shefey chained in the corner began to cry and the sound roused the sleeping demon. Grumbling in ferocious Dlalth, he reached for the nearest object at hand, grasped a large metal flagon, and hurled it savagely at the youngling without ever bothering to open his eyes. The flagon bounced off the floor at the little shefey's feet and smashed into the post that secured her chains, missing her by only a few inches. This further evidence of the abhorrent treatment she suffered was more than Ilys could bear. Hissing like a viper, she spread her wings wide, then closed them forcefully to make use of the forward momentum this action produced to propel her at the cursing Centurion. The blade she brandished sank into his throat just below his chin and, although he floundered and grappled in search of the foe bearing down on him, the blood pouring down his throat hindered his retaliation. Grasping hold of the massive horns protruding from his forehead, Ilys leaned back, beating her wings in a furious backward motion to increase her weight as she yanked his head back and opened the wound in his throat, effectively drowning him in his own blood.

The massive Reviled One thrashed blindly, scratching at the hands that were wrapped around his horns while he rasped and gurgled grotesquely, but it took less than a minute for the traumatic loss of blood he suffered to subdue him. When he finally ceased to struggle, Ilys straightened and glared down with absolute hatred at the twisted face she recognized only *too* well. He had been a Centurion a long time and had been part of her own Integration, but he would never hurt another living being again. Hissing loudly at the wide-eyed, gaping expression frozen upon his now lifeless features, she sprang onto him where he lay sprawled upon the blood-stained cot and, using the heel of her boot, pressed the dagger down into his throat until it nearly disappeared.

Standing on his chest, she looked up suddenly and peered out of the tent to the roadway where two Legionnaires had stopped to stare at the black tent. Cursing under her breath at the commotion she had unwittingly caused, she hopped down from her quarry, snatched the ring of keys he wore upon his belt, and turned to face the small childfey huddled in the corner. Raising her hands in a gesture meant to calm her, Ilys forgot about the blood staining her pallid white complexion and the sight caused the childfey to squeal in horror and bury her head in arms. Looking round her hastily for something with which to wipe the blood away, Ilys stooped to pick up a shredded article of clothing from the floor and cleaned her hands with it in a rush. Outside, the pair of Legionnaires changed direction and moved closer to the tent even as she tossed the blood-stained rag onto the Centurion with a defiant glare and turned back to the childfey.

* * *

The track that led to the Braying Caverns was little more than a narrow, parched trail that was hemmed in on one side by high cliff walls that ramped upward steeply. It was bordered on the other side by a sheer, vertical drop more than one hundred yards in depth. At the base of this embankment, razor-sharp rocks stretched outward, declaring in unmistakable language that the slightest misstep meant certain death. The three Liberators ran along the base of the high cliff wall, keeping as close to its security as they could while searching the ashen dimness for obstacles in their path. Perils lay everywhere in the form of boulders that had fallen from the heights and now lay in heaps of rocky debris along the trail. There were ruts and holes that yawned perilously just waiting to send a passerby tumbling, and straggling ropes of vines snaked across the path, reaching to entangle themselves round ankles.

Standing In Shadows

In the lead, Gairynzvl utilized a well-practiced gait to traverse the harsh terrain by half running and half flying. Flexing his wings repeatedly with a precisely controlled motion, the resulting wing beats provided just enough lift to keep him from stumbling. Following behind him, Ayla and Evondair encountered greater difficulty in negotiating the stony, rutted pathway. More than once Ayla caught her feet on an unseen obstruction and several times the Healer had to slow his pace in order to prevent himself from sprawling onto the dusty trail. Nevertheless, they reached the entrance to the caverns only moments after Gairynzvl, which allowed him just enough time to orient himself.

He had been to the Braying Caverns on several previous occasions, not only during his own Integration when he had been abandoned in the vast network of caves and hollows for endless days, but also as a young Legionnaire. Then, he had been forced to commit acts of such savagery against other younglings and childfey that the memories still painfully tormented his mind. Stopping in the broad opening of the cavern, he peered through the bars of the rusted gate that blocked the entrance and searched the silent blackness. He felt suddenly irresolute about reaching out with his senses into dark environs. He knew the caverns would be saturated with unimaginable suffering and that raw emotion could easily overwhelm him. When Evondair and Ayla drew close beside him to gaze hesitantly inward as well, he turned his head to look down at her, unable to disguise the uncertainty in his lavender-ice gaze.

The moment he had been planning for years had arrived, yet, now that it was upon him, he dreaded taking a single step forward. The memory of their shared nightmare lingered vividly in his thoughts, as did his own painful remembrances, which were made even more unbearable by returning to the place from which they spawned. Reaching for her physically, he sought the consolation of her touch and the buoying effect of her positive essence as the weight of unnumbered torments began to bear down on him. Looking up at him with reservations similar to his own betrayed though the glimmer in her amber eyes, she heard the echoes of The Elders in her thoughts.

"Will you stand by Gairynzvl, even in the depths of Darkness? Will you aid him, even in the face of fear, evil, danger?"

The questions filtered into his mind as she remembered and she nodded up at him, tightening her grasp upon his hand. "Yes. I will." She answered aloud, the sound of her soft voice muffled against the penetrating darkness leeching from the cavern before them, but the warmth of her small hand in his and her optimism that glimmered in her golden aura, even in that dark place, renewed his confidence. Releasing her hand, he stepped back from the ancient, rusting gate barring their way and gazed at the corroded lock, wondering fleetingly how long it had hung there unopened by any key. Raising his hand, he assumed a stance of resolute determination much as he had done before opening the portal in the Room of Transition and with an indomitable tone, spoke the incantation to release the spell sealing the Braying Cavern's gate.

"Hchrynoch thalinan vrask golna cheum!" At the sound of his commanding voice, the gate shook violently, then juddered open. Gazing across at his companions with obvious hesitation, he could see a similar mixture of surprise and trepidation plainly evident upon their faces. Drawing a deep breath, he stepped into the dimness of the cavern. Immediately he noticed that the dusty gravel underfoot became sticky with mud and the air turned heavy with musty dampness and permeating cold. Ayla followed him closely, reaching to take his hand again as the gloom robbed her of clear vision and the thick air stole her breath. The suffocating sensation created by the heavy atmosphere made all of them breathe more deeply. As they drew closer together Evondair paused, observing his companions with keen interest evident in the depths of his brilliant viridian eyes. They stopped, closed their eyes in unison and opened their minds to the shadows.

Darkness and silence filled the cave, seeping into their thoughts like a terrifying chill. The only sound escaping the clinging murk was the occasional drip of water from a source unseen and the slurk of mud beneath their boots. Gairynzvl continued forward into the blackness, stretching out his free hand while supporting Ayla with the other. His thoughts filled with images far more ghastly than their nightmare had conjured and each time he paused to glance over his shoulder towards the gate in order to reorient himself, he could not keep from covering his face or shaking his head in a futile attempt to ward off the horrifying imagery assaulting him.

Without warning, sounds of desolate weeping filled the cavern, echoing from the depths of obscurity, and the emotion that pummeled into them was so intense, so wretched, so devastating, that Ayla wailed at its brutal touch. Gairynzvl released her hand to draw his arms and wings over his head in a vain effort to shield himself while he groaned in physical pain. Within the deepest recesses of his mind he could hear the same sound of hopeless weeping, but it was not the childfey around them whom he sensed. The sound he heard was the memory of his own Integration, a recollection of the many times he had cried in despair as a youngling. These unbearable memories mingled with the sounds encircling them with agonizing clarity and even as he fought to clear his senses, the taste of salt tears filled his mouth.

Behind them, Evondair watched through the duskiness of the cavern with a fixed stare, certain they were not only reliving the horrifying details of the nightmare they had shared, but that those events were now unfolding in the present. Around them, the blackness breathed with soft whispers and gasps. The empty vastness of the cavern resonated subtly with pattering footsteps and shadows crept from the bleakness to surround them. The shadows were small and clustered together in groups, whispering nearly indiscernibly as they drew closer and, in spite of the fact that he was neither telepathic nor empathic, the Healer knew with certainty that the dark shapes congregating around them were not figments of his imagination.

They had found the childfey.

Uncovering his head, Gairynzvl peered into the darkness and stepped forward once again, slowly reaching out with his hands to touch that which he sensed. Countless memories and whispers swirled through his thoughts and he was not alarmed when he felt feathered wingtips, matted hair, grimy clothing and the delicate contact of tiny fingers reaching out for him. Drawing a shuddering breath overflowing with emotion, he turned to locate Ayla. Desperately he whispered to her through his thoughts that she should not open her mind to them even as Evondair moved closer in the shuffling dimness and spoke nearly the exact same warning to her. "Ayla, protect yourself. Do not reach out."

Crouching down in the mud of the cavern, Ayla withheld the sensitivity of her empathy, but she could not refuse the tenderness of her heart. Reaching outward with open arms to the childfey whom she knew had been drawn to them from the shadows, she could not silence herself from whispering softly to them that it would be all right. She was unprepared, however, for the mob of hands and wings and little bodies that pressed so close to her that she was unable to keep her balance in the treacherous mud. Her feet slipped and slid beneath her and her hair was pulled. Her wings were tugged in opposite directions at once and she was jostled chaotically. Had Evondair not reached down through the shadows to yank her upwards, she would have been overrun by younglings rushing forward who were desperate for the warmth of a gentle touch.

"You must be wary, Ayla. They are childfey, but they are so neglected they will harm you without realizing." He reminded her with a firm edge in his voice. Ayla stifled a gasp, attempting to regain her senses. He held her tightly, not only to steady her equilibrium, but to prevent her from taking any additional actions that might pose a threat. Watching wordlessly, Gairynzvl stared at them with a muddled expression. He was unaccustomed to the rush of emotions that flooded over and through him with memories that were so inescapable he could not combat the tide. In her own state of dismay, Ayla did not notice his bewilderment, but gazed round her at the huddling mass of shadows encircling them and for a brief, terrifying moment she felt adrift upon a mighty torrent.

Reaching forward, Evondair held onto Ayla with one hand and sought to pull Gairynzvl closer with his other, but the result of physically joining initiated a startling and wholly unanticipated shared awareness that left them staring at each other with astonishment. In that instant, Evondair was swallowed up by a chaos of pain-filled cries and wails of grief; of shouts and growls so intimidating he shook at the sound. The echoes of weeping that filled his mind seemed to match the keening emitted by The Elders in the Devotionary. At the same time the Healer fought this bewildering swirl of emotion, Gairynzvl sensed a placidness of serenity he had never experienced before. A balm of peacefulness washed over him like a gentle zephyr on a warm summer evening and the absolute horror that had been threatening to pitch him into madness, swiftly abated. Ayla stood between the malefey, turning her head to gaze from one to the other as the Healer's gentle essence soothed and the Fierce One's tenacity and strength of purpose renewed her own.

Standing together amidst a surging ocean of wailing and misery where pain reached out with small hands to pull them down into the precipitous well of despair, the three Fey of the Light gazed at each other with far greater understanding of their Purpose than any of them had ever benefited from before. And in that moment of clarified perception, the light at the mouth of the cavern shifted.

Chapter Nineteen

Panicked shrieks and screams pierced the silence of the Braying Caverns as the childfey who were clustered around the Fey of the Light caught sight of a tall she-Demon standing in the entrance of the cave, peering in through the rusted bars of the gate. Her silvery horns protruded through the bars and she wore a strange mask over her mouth and nose lending her an even more ferocious appearance. Racing back into the shadows, the younglings retreated like a flock of frightened sheep and with their withdrawal the dreadfulness of their conveyed emotions diminished.

"Rynzvl!" The voice was Ilys', but it was mutated somehow, made deeper and more resonant by the mask she wore.

Ayla turned to look up at Gairynzvl. "Rynzvl?" She repeated doubtfully, but, although he hissed with annoyance at this unanticipated discovery, he only shook his head and moved back towards the gate to once again release the spell of binding perpetually cast upon it. In his absence, Evondair and Ayla glanced incredulously at each other, but said nothing.

"How did you get here so quickly?" he asked as Ilys stepped into the dank environment followed by Mardan, Bryth and Reydan. She scoffed at his question, reaching to remove the mask covering half her face while the malefey behind her did likewise.

"Tox-guards, of course." Twirling the protective mask on her finger, she answered in the same saucy tone she had used when she first appeared to him in the corridor of the Temple, playfully taunting him as if he ought to know better than to ask a question with so obvious an answer. He ignored her teasing, however, and gazed behind her at the malefey.

"Where is the little one?"

She winced at his further inquiry, but turned to point outward at the path just beyond the gates. "Rehstaed has her. When she saw where we were going, she became distressed. He is trying to explain things to her."

Gairynzvl nodded.

"Have you found the childfey?" Mardan queried impatiently, stepping forward while shaking the soot and filth that had accumulated on his wings and in his hair during their brief flight from the portal. Gairynzvl nodded again and turned to gesture into the shadowy darkness.

"They fled back into the shadows when they saw Ilys."

An impish sneer twisted the corner of Mardan's smile. "Understandably."

Glancing at each other undecidedly, the Celebrant and she-Demon shared a contemplative gaze, but only for an instant before she turned back to Gairynzvl and suggested that he open the gate once more in order to let Rehstaed and the little shefey inside.

"Why? We will be going back out in just a moment. I only have to call the childfey," he began with confusion, but before he could continue, she interrupted.

"Here's the thing, we cannot go back to the portal," she advised matter-of-factly. Her unexpected statement drew inquiries from all of them and they moved closer to hear her reply more clearly in the muffled thickness of the cavern's dense atmosphere.

"What?"

"Why not?"

"What have you done?" Gairynzvl's tone bristled with annoyed expectation as he already feared what she might say. Glancing away from him with a fleetingly guilty expression, she shrugged and answered in a halting manner that betrayed her culpability.

"I may have killed the Centurion."

Shocked gazes answered her confession.

"You killed the Centurion?" Disbelief filled every word of Gairynzvl's repetition, causing her to hastily add to her admission.

"He woke up. It was unavoidable."

"You said none would see you!" Mardan retorted, his irascible nature swiftly replacing the fleeting curiosity he felt about her. She turned to glare at him, but before she could hurl any retaliatory insults upon him, Bryth spoke with a tone of certainty that none could dispute.

"The entire Legion will be searching for his killer."

Staring at her for a protracted moment without making a sound, Gairynzvl then strode beyond the group and back to the gate where he repeated the incantation to release the spell that kept its rust-sealed lock permanently closed. Stepping into the threshold, he searched the gloom in the direction of the encampment and as he did, Rehstaed moved closer carrying in his strong, yet severely scarred arms the small childling Ilys had liberated.

"There 'as been a great deal o' shoutin' comin' from tha' camp. If we are goin' back to th' portal, we ough' to go."

The Fierce One gazed at him silently, then drew a deep breath and shook his head. Motioning them into the cavern, he secured the gate before responding loud enough so that all who were present could hear him. "Ilys is right. We cannot go back to the portal." His begrudging concession brought a repetition of dismayed exclamations and questions from his comrades. "They are aware of its existence. It will be the first place they guard," he continued more informatively and Rehstaed stepped closer, still holding the childfey.

"An' when they get there, they shall fin' three more bodies." He glanced across at the other malefey and they nodded in agreement with him, the group of them not entirely successful in concealing their shared smirks of satisfaction at having dispatched the drunken Legionnaires they encountered before Ilys returned. Looking down at the little shefey he held with a twinge of apprehension, Rehstaed spoke once more in a more guarded tone. "How, then, shall we get back?"

Icy lavender and piercing violet locked and for a prolonged moment not a single sound pervaded the darkness. Gairynzvl gazed into the blackness of the cavern, attempting to recall if there were any other portals within its labyrinthine tunnels. Behind him, the Fey of the Light stood quietly and waited. Ilys stepped backward toward the gate, listening intently for any indication that Legionnaires were heading in their direction and Evondair gazed contemplatively at Mardan. Bryth shook his head wordlessly at Reydan and in the stillness, a single whisper was heard.

"The gate."

Barely able to perceive the softly spoken word, Gairynzvl shifted his stance in an attempt to face the unseen speaker. Raising his hands to his ears as he had done in the vast wasteland outside the encampment, he tried to listen more intently.

Stillness.

Quiet.

An intermittent drip of water pealed through the hushed cavern.

Nothingness.

Frustrated, he drew a deep breath and opened his mind, reaching out in search of the childling who had spoken. Softly he asked through seeking thought alone and waited in silence so heavy it seemed to suffocate him. After a silence that seemed interminable, an answer came back to him.

"The gate."

"The Gate!"

"THE GATE!"

Whispers penetrated his thoughts with the concentrated energy of what sounded like a thousand minds. The voices pressed in on him from the blackness with such abrupt potency that he instantly covered his ears and doubled over in shock, the force of the united thoughts stabbing at him like a blade. Crying out at the unexpected assault, his actions drew his friends close to him and without considering any other alternative Ayla reached for Evondair. He took her hand with a nod of comprehension and they both laid a hand upon Gairynzvl while he twisted and wrapped his wings about himself in distress as he tried to escape the unrelenting torrent of whispers shouting louder and louder in his mind.

"The gate."

"The Gate!"

"THE GATE!"

At the touch of their hands upon his back, Gairynzvl paused and drew a deeply ragged breath, as if the influence of so many minds had stifled his ability to breathe. Ayla closed her eyes and allowed the torment he felt to wash over her. She did not react with wails or tears, however, but stood with astonishing serenity as the brunt of the childlings inadvertent attack was deflected. Conversely, Evondair doubled over and screamed.

The horrifying sound shattered through the vast complex of caverns, sending peals of echoes in all directions. The sound of his solitary voice became an inharmonious chorus as it faded into oblivion, but his honest expression of the emotion he felt rushing from the childfey with the force of a cataclysmic flood broke through their group psychosis and shattered the vehemence of their thoughts. Recovering his senses, Gairynzvl straightened and reached out for

Evondair, placing his hand upon the Healer's shoulder and listening for his thoughts, but the quiet serenity of his essence had returned and he stood up slowly to gaze back at the Fierce One fixedly. Having felt the rush of emotion from the childfey around them, Evondair now understood what Gairynzvl had suffered when he was abducted by the Reviled and this clearer understanding of his misery engendered a far greater respect for him.

"We can return to Hwyndarin through the Great Gate." Gairynzvl announced, turning to face the remaining Liberators, he spoke confidently, but Mardan shook his head. Uncertain, a skeptical frown furrowed his brow, but before he could voice his reservations, Rehstaed asked what none of them believed.

"The Gate o' th' Uunglarda itself? Do you say it really exists?"

Ilys returned from the entrance to the caverns and confirmed that it did with a brusque 'of course' and added pessimistically that it lay many miles in the distance through a system of winding and often perplexing tunnels.

"We have no other choice?" Reydan inquired further, receiving a negating shake of the head from Gairynzvl, as well as from Ilys, as an answer.

He added as an afterthought, as if to try to convince them, "I have been there once."

"Once?" Bryth's apprehension was shared by those around him as they looked at each other hesitantly.

Mardan pressed his point further. "How long ago? Can you remember the way? The last thing we need is to get lost in this place."

Gairynzvl turned to gaze at the far wall of the cavern where he remembered that a tunnel led into the blackness. Searching his memory for the path he had followed only once in his life, he was unprepared for the realization that even more childfey were hiding in the shadows beyond the cavern they stood in, debating. "I could if I could see it, but my eyes are no longer suited to darkness."

His comrades glanced at each other with even greater hesitation, unwilling to venture into the blackness with a guide who was as hampered by the lack of light as they were, but Evondair smiled. From the belt of his pack hung a small leather bag, which he opened carefully to withdraw the item it contained. Turning to face them, he held out a small glass vessel that glowed faintly whitish-blue in the cavernous gloom. "This will aid you." The confidence of his tone and the sight of the glimmering object he held made his companions gasp, but Gairynzvl stared at the ornate little bottle with bewilderment. Ilys drew closer to peek around Mardan's broad shoulder and wing to gaze at it with similar astonishment.

"What is it?" she asked softly, unable to suppress her curiosity.

Evondair's smile widened and he held the vessel up for all to see. "It is a Luxanary. A small lamp containing a phosphorescent mineral found in the ancient mines of Lundoon. The mineral is extremely scarce and very costly to obtain, but one of the Elders brought this back with him after he studied in the lands to the east." As he gave this explanation, Mardan nodded in agreement, having seen the priceless Luxanary on only one other occasion during his years of study at The Temple.

"Zraylaunyth gave this to me before we left the Healing Wards for the Room of Transition." Evondair explained further. His use of the youngest of the Elder's name surprised the group even more than the sight of the extraordinary object he held in his hands and Gairynzvl cocked his head to the side curiously.

"Zraylaunyth?"

Evondair nodded. "The Third Elder. He who Sees."

Nodding at his clarification, Gairynzvl took a step towards the back of the cavern. With the introduction of the Luxanary, their trek through the vast network of tunnels became less daunting and the Liberators prepared to set off. Turning to Mardan. Evondair handed him the Luxanarye ven while Gairynzvl moved quietly into the darkness. He whispered to the childfey he knew were huddled around him in order to communicate their intentions as the Healer and Celebrant discussed their only source of light.

"You are gifted with spells and incantations," Evondair spoke quietly, aware of the Celebrant's hesitancy to use the gift of magic he possessed. "Do you know the illumination spell to amplify its glowing?"

Mardan looked down at the object in surprise, never anticipating he might hold or be permitted to utilize such an invaluable treasure. He considered for a protracted moment, certain he had at some point during his education learned the spell to which Evondair referred. Smiling, he nodded then and spoke the enchantment quietly in the echoing darkness. "Luxaunyth sha-lindauwyn. Vas hevauthycaera."

Ignite Shimmering Light, Hear my Voice. Evondair listened carefully, committing the incantation spoken in High Celebrae to memory in the event he might need to use it again. In response to Mardan's softly spoken words, the

Luxanary's radiance increased like a candle gaining luminosity after being lit. When Mardan repeated the spell, the light it produced increased once again.

"Should you need to diminish its glow, you simply say: 'Suubsyydd.'" With his word the Luxanary's light faded, although it did not extinguish itself completely. Nodding with comprehension of how to use these simple spells, Evondair received the vessel back from the Celebrant before he moved towards the front of the group where Gairynzvl waited.

After increasing the light of the Luxanary, they stepped forward into the darkness that was now bathed in a bluish-white, spectral glow. As they approached the back of the cavern where a narrow tunnel snaked away into the distance, the Fey of the Light were able to see for the first time the clusters of timorous childfey pressed against the back wall. Their pale complexions were made ghostly in the phosphorescent glimmering and they winked and winced in the unnatural light, their eyes already becoming accustomed to darkness. Some of their gazes already glowed red from within, indicating the alteration from Fey of the Light to Reviled had already begun.

Noticing this, Ayla queried in a hushed tone, "Should they all follow us? What if some of these childfey are dangerous, like you explained to us in the garden room?"

At hearing her question, Gairynzvl stopped and turned around to stare back at her with a pained expression. He was certain she was correct, that each of the childfey should have been read in order to gauge their volatility, but he could not force himself to leave any of them behind. He made a feeble excuse. "We should, but there is no time, Ayla."

Glancing past him towards the clusters of childfey, the fear and uncertainty he could see in her gaze compelling him to add to his reply with greater honesty. "Can you tell them not to follow us? Could you bear leaving any of them behind?"

She could not answer his questions and when his searching stare met hers, she could only shake her head in answer. Outside the cavern in the direction of the encampment, the distant echo of a garish horn call sank into the gloom like a blade.

Chapter Twenty

The labyrinth of passageways and twisting corridors was more bewildering than Gairynzvl could ever have remembered. Thick blackness lurked around every turn and at each intersection of tunnels the emptiness sucked at the light they carried as if it were a living entity drawing vitality from the glimmer and endeavoring to strand them in utter darkness. Without the light, they would surely have been lost. Even Ilys could not see in total blackness and as soon as they left the main cavern any hint of illumination from outside was devoured by the ravenous darkness.

    Followed at some distance by a growing group of childfey, who crept out of dark corridors and from behind the safety of large boulders to join the group as they passed, the Liberators proceeded in pairs. Trusting Gairynzvl more completely than any of them might have imagined they would in spite of only knowing him so short a time, the Fey of the Light walked in complete darkness for the first time in most of their lives. With Evondair at his side and Ayla just behind him, the former Dark One moved along the passageways tentatively, certain he had walked the same route before, although the incandescent light illuminating the way beguiled his memory. In the blue-white radiance the stony walls, lowering ceilings and mud-smeared floors all looked the same. Many times he twisted around in doubt of the way and more than a few times, he stopped and walked back along the waiting group as he double-checked that he had taken the right route. As they passed by yawning spans that stretched into nothingness and pitch black openings leading into obscurity, he paused to look round him uncertainly or he took hold of the Luxanary to step inward cautiously as he attempted to remember which way was correct.

With each hesitation, the trepidation of the group became more palpable. Behind the straggling cluster of childfey, Ilys brought up the rear. She was unafraid of the darkness and could see best in the minimal illumination. Although the gate to the caverns was sealed, she felt certain there would be at least one Legionnaire among the ranks of the Centurion who knew the incantation required to release the lock. In that case, she could bend light around the back of the group and, hopefully, mislead any who pursued. Lingering behind the group, she listened intently for any sounds coming from the direction of the opening of the cavern and when the dissonant blare of a Dlalth bugle echoed along the corridors she gasped in alarm and hurried forward to the closest childfey.

Bending closer as they trudged along, she spoke in a hushed, but urgent tone. "You must warn our leader that we are being followed," she told the youngling insistently, but the little one squealed in terror at the she-Demon's nearness and wriggled away from her into the safety of the group. Frustrated, she moved to the next, a small boyfey whose wings had been stripped nearly bare of feathers in some heartless form of punishment. "Please do not fear me," she whispered to him gently and he stopped to look up at her. His face was disfigured by sunken eyes and hollow cheeks, his clothing hung on him in soiled tatters, his limbs were thin from starvation and his bare little feet were caked with thick mud. Pained by the sight of him, she stooped to embrace him and drew him up to carry him. In spite of the untold horrors he had suffered at the hands of other Demonfey, the childling wrapped his arms about her neck and clung to her, his trust and more than obvious need for any form of kindness sending a pang of emotion through her. Stifling the onslaught of this poignant sentiment, Ilys smiled sympathetically at him and whispered her plea once again. "We must warn our leader that we are being followed. Can you talk to him with your thoughts?"

The boyfey shook his head, but pointed at a little shefey further ahead of them in the group. "Dynnzl can, but she is not supposed to," he said with certainty and Ilys nodded, pushing forward through the straggling younglings in spite of his cryptic warning and carrying the little boyfey with her as she went.

* * *

Standing at a crossways of three separate tunnels, Gairynzvl sighed sharply with exasperation. He was hungry; he was tired; his eyes hurt from the strange blue light illuminating their way, and he had no idea which way to go. Beside him, Evondair also sighed.

"Perhaps we should take a short break?" he suggested in a concerned tone. "Some food and a bit of Quiroth will make a vast difference for all."

Closing his eyes to cover them with the heels of his hands, Gairynzvl willingly agreed and at his nod, the Healer turned to tell the others. A multitude of relieved sighs met his pronouncement and the train of footsteps slowly halted. It took only a few moments for the Fey of the Light to remove loaves of hearty bread, rosy apples and small wheels of cheese from their packs. Sitting down amid clusters of impatient childfey, they shared a meager meal. It was the first food some of the childfey had seen in days and they pushed forward eagerly with ravenous hunger. Bottles of invigorating Quiroth were opened and the dark, earthy liquid was poured over small pieces of bread and given it to the younglings to fortify them. A piece of bread, one bite of an apple and a crumble of cheese was not much, but it was all they had and only when all the little ones had eaten something did the Liberators partake as well.

Rynzvl! They are coming!

An unexpected thought pierced Gairynzvl's mind, penetrating his consciousness from the darkness, but he understood the warning and recognized instantly from whom it had come, despite the fact that the message was delivered through the thoughts of a childling. Squeezing his eyes closed in an attempt to block the repeating whisper stabbing into him like a blade, he filled his mind with the single answer that he understood and, to his great relief, the knife-like telepathy stopped.

"What is it?" Ayla asked softly, raising her hand to touch his shoulder lightly. She had prudently blocked her own mental acuity for the sake of protection, but blocking the perilous telepathy of the childfey left her without the ability to hear his thoughts. He turned to look at her blankly, then gazed outward over the small assembly gathered in the dimly lighted juncture. He knew he had to decide which way to go. He also knew their lives, each and every one of them, depended upon the accuracy of that choice.

He had never been accountable for anyone other than himself. He had never needed to concern himself over the well-being or security of another, but at that moment dozens of lives depended upon him and his ability to guide them to safety. When he had formulated his plan to undergo the Prevailation and then return to the Uunglarda in order to liberate whatever childfey he could find, he had not considered the degree of responsibility such actions might require. Now, when all those around him waited to follow his next action, he felt overwhelmed. What if he was wrong? What if his choice led them into greater peril? His first instinct was to knock away the tenderness of Ayla's offered touch and stalk away into the darkness, either to hide his fear or to try to collect himself, but he realized he could do neither "The Legionnaires are coming and I cannot remember the way."

Aware that she had closed her thoughts in order to protect herself, he spoke as softly as he could form the words, but in spite of his vigilance to be as discreet as possible her honest reaction of startled dismay caught Mardan's attention who was sitting quietly nearby. Unwilling to arouse fear in the others, he got to his feet and moved towards them nonchalantly, bending close and spreading his wings behind him to shield their conversation while he inquired in a hushed tone. "What is wrong? Where is Ilys?"

Gairynzvl looked up at him without raising his head, gritting his teeth to control his frustration. "She is behind the childfey. She sent a message to me through them, through their telepathy, that the Legionnaires are coming. I do not know how close or how far, but we must go."

The look of concern that met this report stung like a horde of angry bees, but instead of reacting confrontationally, as was his nature, Mardan stayed in his cautious position and quietly inquired further. "Which way are we to go? Do you remember?"

Glaring lavender met icy cerulean, but the enmity between them that seemed ready at any moment to erupt into aggression did not propel them into yet another quarrel. Leaning even nearer to speak more confidentially, Mardan said something the former Dark One watching him intensely did not anticipate. "I cannot blame you if you do not remember. I have found myself confused several times just following you through this murk, but we must keep ahead of the Legionnaires. If you are unsure which way to go, you must not *appear* unsure."

Gairynzvl stared at the Celebrant in silence. The Celebrant stared back, unmoving. Between them, Ayla held her breath nervously, but Gairynzvl looked past Mardan's broad white wings at the others. Hesitating briefly, he got up to reconsider the possible routes they could take while Mardan smiled subtly at Ayla and straightened while drawing his wings closed. Gairynzvl stepped towards a narrow aperture situated inconspicuously between two other tunnels that led in opposite directions. Laying his hands upon the walls at either side of this constricted fissure, he peered into the darkness that waited within even as a sly smile turned the corner of his mouth.

The way is not the way, but the way of the wayward.

The riddle repeated itself in his thoughts. He was not at all certain if it was another message from a childling or his own memory of how to find the gate, which he had been told so many years ago that he had forgotten until that moment. Regardless of its source, however; he turned around and urged them to prepare for a more difficult, more confined passageway. He did not openly mention the advance of the Legionnaires, but as the group arranged to set off, he moved towards his fellow Liberators and told them with a hushed tone what he had not shared with the childfey. "The Legionnaires are pursuing. Ilys is at the rear of the group and may require assistance if they follow us to the Great Gate."

Agreeing that they should join her in the event they needed to engage the enemy, the malefey prepared to set off, but Gairynzvl stepped closer and whispered in a low voice so only they could hear him. "Any indication of the Dlalth in our midst will send the childfey scattering in all directions and make all our efforts pointless."

They assured him they would act guardedly before turning towards the rear of the group. Satisfied that he had done what he could, Gairynzvl once again took the lead with Evondair by his side. The crevice into which they had to pass was barely wider than a few feet at its widest points and most of the adult Fey were forced to turn sideways at one time or another in order to squeeze through the constricted passages. The cramped environment reduced the effectiveness of the Luxanary, as its spectral light was blocked by the congestion of bodies lined up in the narrow corridor, leaving most of them to follow in almost complete darkness. As a result, anxiety rose and many of the childfey protested at having to walk blindly through the frightful tunnel, some of them so loudly that even the Liberators at the rear of the group could hear them. Something had to be done. Stopping in frustration, Gairynzvl met Evondair's gaze, but the Healer smiled calmly and reached for the rope that hung from his pack.

"They just need a little security. We can tie our ropes together and each youngling can cling to in order to feel connected with the rest of the group and not become lost." His suggestion was met with an appreciative smile and an extensive length of rope was hastily created and passed down the column of frightened childfey. Evondair moved among them, reassuring them with his innate composure and it only took a few minutes before they were once again ready to proceed.

The restricted fissure led them up steep inclines and around tight corners, twisting and turning in contradictory directions that left all of them disorientated, but they had no alternative. They had to press on as hastily as they could. If Legionnaires were following them inside the Braying Caverns, then time was running out. Aware of the urgency of their situation, Gairynzvl quickened his steps, but shuffling along in the dimness at the pace of a forced march overwhelmed some of the childfey so that they refused to continue onward. Already at the limits of their strength and far beyond their ability to cope with such arduous demands, other little ones who did not stop began to cry and, like the momentum of a relentless tide, their weeping prompted more weeping until nearly all the younglings were squalling loudly.

Sighing sharply with exasperation at the noise they were making, Gairynzvl twisted about with the intention of asking Ayla if she might do something, anything, to bolster their spirits, but as he turned a whisper pierced his conscious mind like a dagger. It's sharp intensity caused him to grimace and groan in pain.

Rynzvl, hurry! Dlalth are everywhere!

Squeezing his eyes tightly closed, he doubled over and covered his head with his arms, vainly attempting to ward off the repeating whisper that serrated through his thoughts like a razor. Evondair watched him for a brief moment in surprise before reaching out to touch him in the hope that he might ease his pain as he had done before. In spite of her efforts to squeeze round the Healer, however, Ayla stood beyond reach and without the blending of their three unique gifts into one touch, the Healer could do nothing. Gritting his teeth against the infiltrative pain of the solitary whisper, Gairynzvl straightened abruptly and arched backward in distress while desperately trying to silence a scream.

"He understands!" Evondair twisted around, the gentle Healer hissing towards the clusters of childfey behind them with an unusually agitated tone. "He hears you, but you must stop before you harm him."

Growling against the pain shattering through his thoughts, Gairynzvl stared blindly at the ceiling, reaching out for the sides of the tunnel to keep from falling as his senses began to spin from the excruciating telepathy slashing through his mind.

"Without him we cannot escape this place!" The Healer shouted with even greater exasperation, watching helplessly as Gairynzvl writhed in torment. Then he gasped profoundly and fell to his knees as the torturous communication that had been forced upon him dissipated as abruptly as it had begun. The sensation of release that washed over him was euphoric and he could not hide the tears of relief that slipped from his eyes when the Healer leaned over him and placed his hand on his shoulder to be certain the telepathy had ceased. Nodding wordlessly, Gairynzvl breathed unsteadily and attempted to get up, but as a result of the trauma he had just experienced from the intensity of the whisper that had torn through his mind, his limbs felt numb and his strength failed him.

"You should rest." Evondair's tone held the calm serenity of a Healer once again, but the tremor in his voice betrayed his dismay. Shaking his head, Gairynzvl tried pushing up from the floor another time, explaining breathlessly that they could not afford to linger for even a moment.

"The Reviled are tracking us. They are within the cavern and closing in. We cannot delay!" At hearing his warning, the golden-haired Fey glanced over his shoulder with noticeable trepidation. His wide-eyed gaze swept over the younglings sniffling around them and, in spite of the noise they were making, he turned back and leaned closer to draw Gairynzvl securely into his arms. With the Healer's strong supportive embrace he finally found his feet, although he stood unsteadily for a moment collecting his senses. Before he could stagger onward, Evondair bid him to wait while he rummaged through the pack Gairynzvl carried between his nebulous wings. Seeking his allotment of Quiroth, which he had not yet utilized, he drew the bottle out and held it out.

"Drink this."

Gairynzvl, who stood staring blankly into the distance in a muddled haze, did not respond. Evondair placed the bottle in his hand, waited and then physically raised his hand to his mouth. "It will strengthen you. Drink!" Again the Healer spoke with a surprisingly forceful tone and Gairynzvl shook himself at last, grasped the bottle more firmly and tilted it hastily over his lips. He remembered the foul tang of the amber liquid from the last time he had been required to drink it and his reaction to the strong, earthy flavor and pungent aroma was the same. Turning his head abruptly, he could not force himself not to spit it out as he groaned in disgust and shuddered with revulsion at its taste, but the Healer would not be eluded so easily. Leaning close another time, he spoke with an unmistakably threatening tone. "Would you like me to call for Mardan? I am sure he would be only too happy to restrain you while I *force* you to drink."

Twisting to gaze backward at the Healer in astonishment, Gairynzvl scoffed, then shook his head when Evondair neither moved away nor said anything further, demonstrating his intractable intentions through the silence of his piercing viridian stare. Raising the bottle to his mouth begrudgingly, Gairynzvl frowned ferociously at it, tilted his head back and drank its contents in one draught. Hissing with loathing at the empty container, he handed it abruptly back to Evondair.

"You will thank me for this." The Healer assured him with an overly-confident and gently jeering tone, but Gairynzvl did not reply. His concentration was entirely focused on the immediate and singular objective of quelling his overwhelming need to retch.

When the violent twisting in his stomach subsided, Gairynzvl drew a deep breath and stepped forward once again. Following the narrow corridor through its twists and turns for the better portion of an hour and fearful that at any moment the strident horn calls of Legionnaires would fill the tunnel behind them, he pushed himself and the younglings who followed him to their limits. With his mind buzzing and his senses still dazed from the painfully intense telepathy forced upon him, he strode ahead through the force of sheer will alone. He listened with mounting apprehension for any sound coming from behind them that might alert him to the presence of the Reviled, but the only noises he heard were the scuffling footsteps of dozens of childfey and their whimpers of exhaustion.

Through the bluish glow of the Luxanary, he could see the tunnel they followed stretching into the distance, an endless, winding passage of bleary color and bewildering bends. As he trudged along, he wondered hazily if he had misled them. Was this really the way? Had he taken the wayward way when it was in fact the wrong way? Which way should he have taken; the way they were following or the way he would have followed if the way they went was not the way they were going? His thoughts began to tangle and twist like the beguiling avenue along which they walked. His vision blurred repeatedly from the monotonous glow of blue light and the inability to focus caused him to blink determinedly over and over again trying to clear the muffled sensation lingering in his mind. Then he stumbled, pitching forward in the darkness and tumbling to the dusty floor.

Cursing in fluent Dlalth, he gazed with disbelief at the dusty floor of the tunnel beneath him, his mind spinning with fatigue and an immediate rush of vexation at his own clumsiness. Crossly knocking aside Evondair's hand when he reached to offer assistance, he struggled back to his feet unaided and looked about in search of what had caused him to fall, but only the grimy floor illumined in spectral blue met his gaze. Muttering in annoyed Dlalth, he fixed his attention on the path that lay ahead of them and noticed that the pinched corridor they had been following had unexpectedly opened into a broad chamber.

Peering out into the blackness of that vast space, he reached behind him for the Luxanary and held it up to shed its light into the immense void before them. The heavy silence of that place was deafening. Stillness hung over the empty chamber like a smothering cowl. As they stepped out of the fissure into its cavernous chamber, the sounds they made seemed to be swallowed up by the leaden hush. The Liberators gathered round and the childfey who had collapsed to the floor of the chamber in weary silence and Gairynzvl lifted the Luxanary higher, projecting its light further to illuminate as much of the cavern as he could. In a low tone, Evondair spoke the incantation to increase its glow and its peculiar light flooded outward, filling the vacuous space, glinting off the pitch black of the floor and reflecting from its colossal stone walls.

On the far side of the chamber where the enchanted light of the Luxanary could just barely penetrate the ebon shadows, a massive gate wrought of black iron stood in the consuming silence, its impenetrable obstruction utterly barring the way.

Chapter Twenty-One

The wall illumined by the ethereal glow of the Luxanary was not the natural sides of the cavern, but a fortification constructed with huge blocks of grey and black stone that towered upward to meet the ceiling of the cavern overhead and stretched outward to the sides of the cave. It entirely blocked the way. The cavern ceiling was formed of one solid piece of stone; like the base of a mountain resting precariously atop an empty tomb. The floor of the chamber was laid with enormous squares of similarly hued stone and in the center of the mammoth wall before them, fashioned of heavy iron that shimmered in the phosphorescent radiance illuminating it, a massive black gate stood in the darkness.

Beyond the gate, a path strewn with rough gravel led beneath a continuation of the fortified wall, forming yet another tunnel, but where it led was concealed by impenetrable blackness. Standing in the barren cavern, the Fey of the Light stared in horror at the imposing edifice, unable to conceive how they might escape with such a massive barricade across the way. Around them, the ghostly blue shadows wept and whispered in the voices of dozens of exhausted childfey and Gairynzvl could not keep from gazing back at them with a sickening feeling of dread. Had he led them here for nothing? Would all his years of planning and everything they had suffered come to naught because Ilys had foolishly chosen to kill the Centurion and alerted masses of Legionnaires to their presence in the process? Glaring through the dimness at her, he could not conceal the sudden animosity he felt, but his anger was short-lived when the sound he had dreaded hearing since the moment he returned into the Uunglarda filled the cavern.

The discordant blat of a Dlalth horn did not echo through the vast tunnels and avenues of the cavern from the distance, instead it blared from the fissure they had just left and the sound filled them all with terror. Squealing and shrieking in horror, the younglings sought escape like a flock of frightened sheep, converging together into a huddled mass that moved as far from the crevice as they could go, but the cavern had only two means of escape: the gate, which stood impervious, and the tunnel from which growling Dlalth could be heard.

As the childlings circled in an increasing chaos of panic, Ayla dashed forward to Gairynzvl. Unable to combat the mounting trepidation spiraling around them as well as the rancorous hatred and lust for violence emanating from the Dark Ones surging towards them, she sought his strength. The rush of emotion picked her up and swept her away like a leaf on the shoulders of a river in spring flood and she clung to him with eyes tightly closed, struggling to retain her feeble measure of control. When she saw her cowering, Ilys cursed vehemently and shook her head and shouted over the noise converging upon the cavern. "I told you she would crumble!" Then she twisted about to face the fissure and pulled out the bone-handled dagger she carried even as she waved her hand over her head and vanished.

Bryth and Rehstaed raced towards the narrow corridor's aperture with blades at the ready, shouting to Gairynzvl that they would defend the entrance as long as they could. Growling together in a show of fierce bravado, the two Fey Guards motioned for Mardan to join them. He stood uncertainly as his penetrating cerulean gaze shifting from Ayla to the mouth of the fissure where his comrades beckoned him and back again. Watching with mute agitation, he cursed under his breath as the former Dark Fey he had once tried to kill held his love and stared into her eyes with the most intense gaze he had ever seen.

She wailed in distress. Thrashing her head to fend off the blustering emotions pouring over her from every direction at once and Gairynzvl was forced place both his hands upon her temples to still her panicked actions. Sinking his fingers into the lush coils of her spiraling tresses, he shouted at her through his thoughts as well as through words and the conjoined sound permeated the terror that was surging through her. The shock of his voice surrounding her from inside and out was enough to make her pause and when she opened her eyes he captured her with a fixed stare. The icy-lavender hue of his gaze reflected the glowing radiance of the phosphorescent light of the Luxanary and she could do little more than stare back at him with astonishment and terror.

"It will be alright," he whispered into her mind, but she could not believe him. He repeated himself more adamantly, but the swirl of emotion spinning around them was like a maelstrom that pulled her into its vortex. Beside them, Evondair tracked the reeling huddle of childfey while he called for Reydan's help. He sought to gather them and contain their wheeling flight of escape. He was certain the Fierce One leading them would find some means of opening the gate and wanted to ensure the childfey would be safe until he succeeded. Using their open arms and wings spread wide, the two malefey herded the screeching little ones away from the fissure to prevent any of them from attempting to escape down its now deadly passage. Hushing their cries of fear with words spoken in calming tones, the Healer and gentle musician followed the surging mass in one direction and then another, leading them slowly in the direction they wanted them to go.

Vengeful hissing resonated from the narrow tunnel they had just left as all the Reviled Fey waiting in the blackness joined their voices to create a sound so foreboding that blood ran cold. It was the sound of a demon with the ferocity of a dragon and the implacable resolve of the Lost. Then, from the depths of the shadows, a grisly voice called with taunting patience. "Gairynzvl."

Turning sharply at the unexpected voice, he stared at the hissing passage with dismay. How could they know with certainty that he was there? How were they able to find them so quickly? Frowning with even greater resentment, he realized they could not; not unless someone had told them!

"Gairynzvl."

He saw Ayla close her eyes as tears slipped down her pale cheeks. In spite of the treachery laying ruin to his plans and regardless of the wrenching horror in the pit of his stomach that twisted into a knot when he considered the torture he would suffer for his treason and the unspeakable things they would do to her if they were captured, he looked down at her with greater determination. He heard his friends and fellow Liberators shouting at the opening of the tunnel in a rousing battle cry and felt the weight of the watchful glare of the Celebrant from whom he had unwittingly stolen the beautiful shefey now held in his arms. He recalled the words of the Elders who had asked him to share his strength with her when she had none and he knew this was the moment they had foreseen. Shaking her more firmly, he allowed his stare to melt through her when she opened her eyes once more. "You must be brave, Ayla," he whispered reassuringly, "I will not fail you."

The purposeful tone of his deep voice mingled with the affirming whisper echoing in her thoughts, the intensity of his penetrating stare and the warmth of his virile presence. Terror spiraled around them as the guttural repetition of his name filled the cavern again and again in a tactic of undeniable intimidation. Fear grasped and clawed at her from every angle until the only thing she could do was shiver and weep in unrelenting distress, but Gairynzvl stared at her with a gaze that conveyed every measure of the passion and affection he felt for her. Moving closer, he drew her to him and, although he did nothing more than stare, the beguiling sensations he sent washing over her broke through the fear that suffocated her so thoroughly. Staring back at him with helpless surrender as he cleared away the terror staining her every thought with blackness, she felt his sense of purpose and the tenacity of his essence replacing her unrelenting dread and it revitalized her until, at last, she closed her eyes and smiled dimly.

Growling with resentment at the evident passion he saw in the Fierce One's gaze, Mardan raised his sword and pointed it at them, shouting to be heard over the rising cacophony of noise pouring from the fissure. "Can you open the portal?"

Looking beyond Ayla without lifting his head, Gairynzvl released her and fixed his stare on the Celebrant who stood glaring back at him. "It is not a portal," he answered unhelpfully, setting his wings with determination as he moved away from her and the Luxanary that Evondair had placed on the floor near his feet as he walked into the ethereal blue shadows on the opposite side of the cavern. Mardan watched him in confusion.

"How, then, do you open it?" His question never received an answer. Abruptly the hissing from the tunnel stopped and the ponderous silence drew the Celebrant's attention. As he stared into the shadow of the crevice, every Legionnaire hidden in it's shadows began shouting.

"TRAITOR!"

"Death to Gairynzvl!"

"Death to them All!"

Cowering childfey scattered at the uproar, screeching in terror and running in all directions. Evondair and Reydan split up, attempting to gather them from two fronts and herd them back into one group. As they rushed after them, a single crimson arrow shot out of the fissure, scathing past Rehstaed so closely that his bronze feathers rustled at its passing. It shot into the center of the cavern, skittering across the floor at Ayla's feet and shook her from her empathic trance at last. Grasping the Luxanary, she ran towards a cluster of childfey, hoping its reassuring glow might draw them back together. Another arrow hissed out

Standing In Shadows

of the dark corridor just as Mardan reached Bryth's side; then another; then three more.

The shriek of a youngling shattered the darkness as the blood stained arrow found a victim and the heart-breaking cry was echoed by sadistic laughter. Mardan turned to locate the wounded childling, shouting to Ayla and pointing to the shadows on the far side of the cavern where the little one had taken shelter. As she rushed to help him, another volley of arrows hissed through the opening of the fissure and, although the Fey Guard swung their swords at them in an effort to deflect their trajectory, another wail of pain cut through the darkness as the blood red arrow found its mark.

"Shields!" Bryth shouted. Gathering on either side of the aperture and holding their broad shields at the edges, the malefey managed to cover a large portion of the crevice from which crimson death rained, but, while this ploy effectively blocked their ability to kill from a distance, it also enraged the Legionnaires. Mutters of vulgar Dlalth filled the darkness and with viperous laughter, one of the subordinates was hurled through the opening; his flailing dragon-hide wings and limbs sending the shields scattering as he tumbled out into the blue-white light of the chamber.

Hearing this commotion, Gairynzvl turned his head to watch as Rehstaed drew back his sword and utilized one precise swing to sever the Legionnaire's head from his body. Curses in Dlalth answered this retaliation and, with terrifying growls and hisses the Legionnaires rushed into the cavern one after the other. They were greeted by the keen edges of Fey Guard blades and the skirl of metal upon metal rang through the shadows. Bright Celebrae turned fierce in anger. Curses in Dlalth as well as Rehstaed's peculiar language echoed round the chamber and as the battle raged Gairynzvl turned back to stare at the gate before him with monumental uncertainty.

Rearing up to a height of a dozen feet or more, the gate forged of heavy wrought iron was secured to the stone blocks of the wall on either side with enormous iron bolts. It did not open in the center and swing outward like a pair of doors. It did not open at all. It was fashioned in one piece, its iron twisting in elaborate spirals, curling in ornate circles and fanning out like leaves. To ensure its impassability, the ironwork of the heavy gate had razor-sharp blades forged into its spiraling rods and bars. It did not have a lock upon it that could be undone by magic. It was constructed to stand as an impenetrable barrier between the Realm of the Reviled Fey of the Uunglarda and the Free Lands under the Sovereignty of the Fey of the Light.

Behind him, weaponry clashed and screams echoed; arrows stained crimson in the blood of former victims shot through the darkness and childfey shrieked in terror. Then Ayla's voice pierced the raucous din. Twisting about another time, Gairynzvl watched with mounting anger as several Legionnaires circled around her, forming a ring with their wings and arms and weapons to barricade her and hem her in. Other Dark Ones were harassing small clusters of childfey who had broken from the huddled mass protected behind the expansive wings of the Healer. Reydan had engaged one of the Legionnaires who was holding his sword in one hand and a small toddlefey in his other. The squalling youngling dangled from one arm as the Legionnaire fought the musician for her. Near the Healer, the glimmering light of the Luxanary blazed out, illuminating everything in its bright blue glow including a peculiar ripple of reflected blue-white light that dropped fleetingly from the ceiling or snaked behind Legionnaires. Unobserved by any except the one who recognized its source, this blurred reflection of light latched onto Dark Ones unexpectedly, leaving broken bones and slashed throats in its wake.

The Fey Guard were under brutal attack as more Legionnaires rushed from the tunnel, swinging swords as they came hurtling through the narrow stricture into the strange, bluish light of the cavern. Bryth was bleeding from a gash over his left eye. Rehstaed was howling in the rage of battle-madness. Mardan had turned to watch the group of Legionnaires circling menacingly around the beautiful shefey in their midst, snatching at her hair, her wings, her limbs; tearing at her clothes, pressing in on her like a pack of wild animals. Growling in fury, Mardan rushed at the unguarded, writhing mass and grasped one Legionnaire by the throat as he hissed a single word at his shocked face.

"Cruciavaeryn!"

The Demonfey howled in agony and crumbled to the ground, scratching at the air ineffectively against the excruciating agony of the Spell of Inflicted Pain cast by the Celebrant Fey Guard. Before the Dark One fell, Mardan snatched another by the collar of his coat, yanked him backward brutally and repeated the spell once again. Ayla tried to run, but another of the Legionnaires took hold of her from behind, placing her in front of him for his own protection and pressing one of the barbs from his dragonhide wings into her throat.

Gairynzvl turned back to the gate, listening in horror to the screams of pain, fear and anger echoing through the chamber that had, only moments before, stood in heavy silence. Slowly, with a sickening dread rising from the pit of his stomach with the same intensity that had taken hold of him after drinking the Quiroth, he raised his hands. Metal clashed and clattered behind him. Screeches of agony from the inflicted Dlalth filled his ears. Wails from the only Fey he ever truly loved pierced his heart, but a far worse sound filtered through the chaos and stabbed at his very essence like a blade. A childfey's cries, forced into an unmistakable rhythm as a Legionnaire took his unimaginable pleasure. Twisting round, Gairynzvl could see the small child held in the Demonfey's brutal clutches and the result of of both seeing and hearing such an inconceivable atrocity ignited a fury within him unlike any he ever felt before.

Raising his hands without fear, he took hold of the iron bars of the gate. Gritting his teeth against the pain of razor-sharp blades pressing into his flesh, he grasped the metal firmly. Ayla cried out behind him; Mardan cursed in surprisingly fluent Dlalth; childfey squalled from every direction, but the sound most keen in his hearing was the cries of the little shefey who could not escape the Legionnaire attacking her. Growling in a rising tide of rage, Gairynzvl tightened his grip upon the iron bars and shook the gate mightily as blood seeped between his fingers.

The heavy gate rattled loudly, yet stood impervious. Closing his eyes, he unfurled his expansive wings to utilize a powerful backward wing beat as he yanked harder upon the unyielding ironwork. The razor-like metal dug deeper into his hands. Cries poured from the cavern behind him and curses were hurled at each other in hatred, but none of this noise blocked the unbearable weeping and screaming of childfey. Beating his wings more powerfully, Gairynzvl leaned backwards and pulled harder than before. The stubborn iron protested noisily, but resisted his efforts.

Unable to bear the sounds surrounding him, Gairynzvl beat his wings more ferociously in a hauling, backward motion as he shook the gate with every measure of strength he possessed. The chaos of screams, suffering, and torment sank into him like a blade as his heightened empathic awareness stretched outward, involuntarily opening him to hear as well as to feel the calamity unraveling around him. It was more than he could endure. Screaming against the unremitting horror crashing over him like a colossal wave that hurled him in a tumbling psychosis of fear and pain and sensations too appalling to abide, Gairynzvl shook the heavy gate with furious desperation.

Without warning, extraordinary warmth spread throughout his body. It both invigorated and reenergized him, building the momentum of his energy with a suddenness that defied explanation. For a moment, he stood perplexed. Then he realized it was the Quiroth taking hold at last. Repositioning his grasp upon the gate, he unified the forceful beating of his wings with the powerful wrenching of his body, leaning back as he pulled and shook and hauled upon the ironwork in an increasingly wrathful frenzy. Screaming against the anguish and revulsion filling his mind and crying from the inescapable, sickening sensations assaulting his body, he unleashed the full fury of fifteen years of torment at the hands of the Reviled.

Suddenly, a thunderous sound pierced the mayhem resounding through the cavern.

The sound was both hollow and heavy and it echoed into the vast hall filled with fighting and fear as loudly as it reverberated into the immutable blackness on the other side of the gate. Pausing his agitated efforts, Gairynzvl watched as the top of the gate leaned perilously inward in a slow progression that made him release the bars and beat his wings backward even more frantically. Scuttling away upon the wing as rapidly as he could manage, he watched the heavy wrought iron gate as it groaned with a tremendous noise. Falling back onto the floor, Gairynzvl scrabbled backward, still beating his wings to speed his escape as the gate pitched forward under the force of its on inertia, tearing out the bolts that connected it to the walls as it fell.

The cacophonous clangor it made when it met the black stone tiles of the floor rang through the cavern with deafening intensity, causing all within the chamber to cover their ears and bend away from the din with shocked dismay. As the gate fell, the thick blackness on the other side of its obstruction wavered, spiraling in concentric circles of shadows and fluttering darkness. The horrendous crash caused many of the Dlalth to howl in surprise and race back into the shadowy fissure, fearing the Fey of the Light were coming through from the other side to destroy them. Those that lingered increased their efforts in a final assault of hatred, but their diminished numbers left them vulnerable. Fey Guard blades dispatched the remaining Dark Ones while Mardan, taking advantage of the surprised Legionnaires momentarily distracted attention, leapt forward, shoved Ayla away from the monster, and raised his hand to cast the Spell of Inflicted Pain another time.

"They will get re-enforcements. We must hurry!" Bryth was shouting. Evondair went behind the group of childfey in order to herd them toward the now open gate, but fear left most of them far beyond rational comprehension. Leaving the scrabbling Dark Fey on the floor where he had fallen, Mardan gathered Ayla into his arms and ensured that she was unharmed before they both turned aside to assist Evondair. The three Inflicted Demonfey squalled and screamed in unrelenting distress, but Mardan would not allow any of the others to mercifully dispatch them, insisting they be left as a warning to the others who would, ultimately, come.

Beside him, Rehstaed look down at the screaming DemonFey and hissed belligerently, but Evondair stepped away from the cluster of childfey he was leading towards the opening portal and regarded the inflicted fey with a pained expression. "Do not leave them to suffer. It is cruel and does not honor your true nature." His viridian gaze pierced Mardan's resolute cerulean and the Celebrant initially shook his head, preparing to argue, but the gentle Healer continued quietly, "they were once childfey, just as these we now rescue."

Looking down at the Dark Ones with confused anger, Mardan raised his hand slowly and spoke in a soft, but determined tone, releasing them from the spell. Their screaming stopped. One rushed away into the darkness like a frightened animal, his howls echoing from the corridor as he ran in the opposite direction. Another grasped for the dagger at his hip, but Rehstaed's boot across his throat quickly convinced him to flee instead. The third rolled onto his back with his dragonhide wings spread wide across the floor. He looked up at the fair Fey standing over him, regarding them with a similarly confused expression as tears fell from his crimson eyes.

Staring up at the open portal before him, Gairynzvl watched in mute bewilderment as the blackness in the center of the tunnel continued to shift, spiraling with greater and greater shades of Light that filtered in from the other side. Weary beyond measure, he struggled to his feet and stood watching as the tunnel brightened with glimmering Light. From the darkness, shapes of trees became visible in the distance and the sweet, clean scent of winter air drifted into the rank, stale chamber.

Turning to look at his friends, Gairynzvl pointed at the opening and the materializing realm on the other side, calling out to the childfey cowering in terrified clusters, standing in the shadows. "Freedom Awaits!"

As the bright, crystalline Light of Jyndari filtered into the spectrally illumined cavern, the childfey's weeping quieted. Guiding them gently, the malefey who had just moments before been slaughtering Dark Ones, steered them toward the opening with tender words and patient actions and the youngling's exhaustion dissipating as the Light touched them. Their cries of pain and terror transformed into squeals of delight and they rushed around the One who had led them to safety, racing for their home.

Standing unmoving as the tide of little ones washed by him, Gairynzvl looked down at his hands with the incoherence of absolute fatigue. Blood was all he could see, but his mind had separated from the pain. Watching as childfey tumbled out of shadows into bright light, he felt a gentle touch take hold of him. Strong arms support him and a reflection of broad, white wings stretched round him as he was guided beyond the threshold into the beautiful winter landscape that waited. "Ayla?" he whispered with what remained of his strength, and from beside him, Mardan quietly reassured him of her safety as they moved outward into the cold of the winter woodland.

He could hear Evondair's voice speaking to someone, but try as he might he could not force his eyes open in the blinding white light now surrounding them. He could also hear the blissful sounds of childfey laughing and squealing in delight. From the distance, he could hear Rehstaed's unusual language. He was speaking softly in the gentlest tones, no doubt to a youngling, but tears filled Gairynzvl's vision and he could not see.

Guiding him forward, Mardan paused briefly to collect a heap of snow and place it carefully into his hands, encouraging him to hold it as long as he could tolerate in order to help abate the flow of blood. Its icy touch made the Fierce One wince, but after a moment he sighed as its soothing coolth eased the burning pain enveloping his hands. Ayla came to help guide him as well, and, in spite of Mardan standing close beside them, she could not keep from leaning close to kiss his cheek with tender affection. Yet, even as he turned his head to receive a more pleasing kiss from her, she sobbed audibly and bid Mardan to come closer so she could embrace and kiss him as well.

Listening with weary delight to the sounds that now surrounded him, Gairynzvl became aware of another that made him turn his head from side to side as he endeavored to hear it more clearly. Indistinct voices drifted upon the fresh, crisp air, drawing closer and becoming more excited as they came. Blinking repeatedly, he shook his head, desperate to see.

Once again, childfey screams filled the air.

Growling with frustration, Gairynzvl turned his wing over his shoulder and pressed his face into its softness to dry his eyes, even as Mardan assured him that all was well. Looking up, he peered into the brightness, his growl fading as he saw long lines of Fey coming out of the woodland they now stood in. Some hesitated, clearly unsure of the ferocious looking group that had emerged from the mountain where no gate or portal existed. Others stopped in overwhelmed amazement, staring with mouths agape at the childfey playing at the stranger's feet.

Then the woodland Fey rushed with abandon towards the group, tears of joy and desperate curiosity mingling with gleeful laughter as they called out names in the hope that one of the younglings might be their very own. The childfey rushed to the Fey of the Light, screaming in desperate relief and clinging to any who might share a gentle touch or a kind word. Some Fey knelt down in the snow, gathering two, three, even four little ones into their arms to hug and kiss them again and again. Others picked younglings up to swing round with them with exhilaration, their laughter as free as the glittering Light shimmering over all of them.

Watching in silence, Gairynzvl smiled. Beside him, Mardan smiled as well, turning to gaze quizzically at the Fierce One for whom he felt both hatred and a brotherly affinity he had not felt before and, in spite of the rivalry that existed between them that he could not yet lay aside, Mardan wrapped one arm around his shoulder. Pulling him close in a hearty, sideways embrace, they shared an uncertain stare and laughed with each other in a rare moment of ease.

Looking about, Gairynzvl sought the other Liberators. Reydan had taken an arrow in his wing and was being tended by Evondair. Beside him, Rehstaed held the little shefey who had fallen victim to the vile Legionnaire. He was rocking her tenderly, singing a soft song to her in his native language of Vrynnyth Gahl. Even Ilys had rematerialized and, although she stood in the shadows beneath the depending bows of a resplendent evergreen, she held a little boyfey with nearly featherless wings close in her arms. Giggles and gurgles and twitterings of little ones filled the quiet clearing like birdsong on a bright morning and

Gairynzvl could not restrain a sudden sigh of absolute relief any more than he could combat the tears that once again filled his vision.

"You are a conundrum, Fierce One." Mardan taunted him lightly before he shook his head and moved away towards a group of little ones playing blissfully in the clean snow.

Rustling feathers and a chilling current of spiraling wind proclaimed the arrival of one upon the wing and Gairynzvl twisted round to see Bryth emerging from the portal. In his hands he carried their scattered shields and his armor was stained crimson with the blood of many. Although they had escaped with the childfey, he was not smiling as the rest of the Liberators were; in fact, as he alighted, he ran towards them with a fierce expression. "You must hasten the little ones away and we must stand guard on this side of the portal."

Gairynzvl turned his head to the side in bewilderment.

"The sound of horn calls from the tunnels are more numerous than I could count." Gazing out over the brilliant light of the clearing, Bryth caught his breath. "The Light is on our side, but The Reviled are coming!"

The End

Dear reader,

We hope you enjoyed reading *Standing in Shadows*. Please take a moment to leave a review, even if it's a short one. Your opinion is important to us.

Discover more books by Cynthia A. Morgan at https://www.nextchapter.pub/authors/cynthia-morgan-fantasy-author

Want to know when one of our books is free or discounted for Kindle? Join the newsletter at http://eepurl.com/bqqB3H

Best regards,

Cynthia A. Morgan and the Next Chapter Team

Story continues in:

Breaking Into The Light by Cynthia A. Morgan

To read the first chapter for free, head to:
https://www.nextchapter.pub/books/breaking-into-the-light

Contents

A Word about Fey Words   viii

Chapter One   1

Chapter Two   7

Chapter Three   13

Chapter Four   20

Chapter Five   27

Chapter Six   36

Chapter Seven   43

Chapter Eight   51

Chapter Nine   57

Chapter Ten   62

Chapter Eleven   71

Chapter Twelve   77

Chapter Thirteen   86

Chapter Fourteen	92
Chapter Fifteen	101
Chapter Sixteen	107
Chapter Seventeen	114
Chapter Eighteen	121
Chapter Nineteen	128
Chapter Twenty	135
Chapter Twenty-One	144

CPSIA information can be obtained
at www.ICGtesting.com
Printed in the USA
BVHW070719080920
588294BV00001B/43